ITALIAN'S STOLEN WIFE

LORRAINE HALL

PRESENTS

Harlequin® PRESENTS™

ISBN-13: 978-1-335-93901-2

Italian's Stolen Wife

Harlequin Enterprises ULC
22 Adelaide St. West, 41st Floor
Toronto, Ontario M5H 4E3, Canada
www.Harlequin.com

Printed in Lithuania

MIX
Paper | Supporting responsible forestry
FSC® C021394
www.fsc.org

Lorraine Hall is a part-time hermit and full-time writer. She was born with an old soul and her head in the clouds, which, it turns out, is the perfect combination to spend her days creating thunderous alpha heroes and the fierce, determined heroines who win their hearts. She lives in a potentially haunted house with her soulmate and rambunctious band of hermits-in-training. When she's not writing romance, she's reading it.

Books by Lorraine Hall

Harlequin Presents

The Prince's Royal Wedding Demand
A Son Hidden from the Sicilian
The Forbidden Princess He Craves
Playing the Sicilian's Game of Revenge
A Diamond for His Defiant Cinderella

Secrets of the Kalyva Crown

Hired for His Royal Revenge
Pregnant at the Palace Altar

Visit the Author Profile page
at Harlequin.com.

For Caitlin, writing partner extraordinaire.

"I am very well aware of who you are, *cara*."

His smile felt like some kind of lethal blow. Francesca could not understand why it should make her feel breathless and devastated.

But she had spent her life in such a state. So she kept her smile in place and waited patiently for Aristide to explain his appearance. Even if her heart seemed to clatter around in her chest like it was no longer tethered. A strange sensation indeed.

"I am afraid there has been a change of plans today," he said at last, his low voice a sleek menace.

Francesca kept her sweet smile in place, her hand relaxed in his grip, her posture perfect. She was an expert at playing her role. Even as panic began to drum its familiar beat through her bloodstream.

"Oh?" she said, as if she was interested in everything he had to say.

No one would change her plans. *No one.* She narrowly resisted curling her free fingers into a fist.

"You will be marrying me instead."

The Diamond Club

Billion-dollar secrets behind every door...

Welcome to The Diamond Club: the world's most exclusive society, open only to the ten richest men and women alive. The suites are opulent. The service is flawless. And privacy is paramount! You'll never see the details of these billionaires' blistering romances in any of the papers—but you can read all about them right here!

All available now!

CHAPTER ONE

FRANCESCA CAMPO SAT in the beautiful suite of Valentino Bonaparte's estate and studied herself in the ornate gilt mirror. She looked perfect. Not a dark hair out of place, not a speck of makeup smudged. The white bridal gown had been made just for her and would look flattering at every angle.

Francesca would accept nothing else. This moment was the culmination of years of hard work. *Desperate, imperative* work. In a few short hours, she would be Francesca Bonaparte.

And she would be *free.*

She was on the cusp of getting everything she'd spent the past four years planning. Escape from her father. *Certain* it was a better situation than the one she'd grown up in. She'd made sure of it.

Maybe Vale was a little…uptight. Aloof. But they understood each other. She had done her due diligence in selecting him. So, Vale would give her everything she needed. Freedom, above all else. Safety, on this beautiful, ancestral tidal island off the coast of Italy. Her father couldn't—and more importantly *wouldn't*—reach her here.

As long as today went off without a hitch. Anxiety twisted in her gut, but this was normal. Every day, really. She'd spent her entire life walking on eggshells around a volatile, violent father whose money made him, essentially, invincible. She had been the pawn he'd moved around the world of his making, molded into perfect, obedient submission—or so he thought.

But he'd had no idea that instead he'd built the kind of person who would one day design her own escape. And no one would ever believe her capable of such pragmatic, single-minded ruthlessness because everyone only saw the flawless image her father had crafted.

Which made her plan perfect.

In the press, she was goodness personified. A veritable *saint* of an heiress to Bertini Campo's impressive fortune. No one had ever been able to find a single flaw—her father had beaten those out of her long ago—and she wouldn't start with flaws on the most important day of her life.

Even now, after so much hard work, it was difficult to believe she'd made it. In the beginning, Francesca had assumed she would have to pretend to fall madly in love with Vale Bonaparte. Fluff his ego and play to his pride and continue to portray the image of exemplary, obedient bride material.

But this had not been the case. Over her months of trying to woo him without letting him *realize* she was trying to do so, she had soon learned that Vale had no interest in passion or romance.

He was looking for a sure deal, and, fortunately, so

was she. They understood each other, would help one another, and that was *that*.

She gave herself one last look in the mirror, took a deep, careful breath and counted as she let it out. Then she fixed on her best, sweet, innocent smile that she would flash at all the guests. Every last onlooker.

No cameras. No one outside the carefully curated guest list. Vale had insisted, and she, being the good, obedient *perfect* fiancée, had agreed. Of course, she wouldn't have minded a *few* pictures. Deep down, she would have rather liked a grand, rollicking party to celebrate her freedom.

But she'd long ago locked up those "deep down" impulses. Besides, this very small, very private wedding was a nice reprieve considering her father usually insisted on every camera he could wield his power over to follow her about, forever growing her reputation as the perfect heiress.

Forever holding her prisoner.

Angelic enough to be acceptable, charitable enough to not be considered vapid. She'd gone to university, proven her intellect so that even whispers of her father buying her grades were laughed off. But she also dressed modestly, smiled, never argued, and made everyone in her orbit feel listened to.

She knew how to wrap *anyone* around her finger, and all the biting her tongue, pretending she was someone else, perfecting a mask that sometimes made her feel dead inside…well, it was all paying off.

She moved to the arched window that looked down over the entrance. The day was sunny and warm beyond her window, and guests were filing in. It was almost here. She was *almost* free.

She saw a woman with a scarf wrapped around part of her face, an odd choice in the warmth of the afternoon. Francesca studied her, something about the woman's half-hidden profile so familiar.

From this distance, Francesca almost ignored it, but then the woman tilted her head just to look around, and Francesca had the image of many, *many* pictures.

This was no ordinary guest. This was *Princess* Carliz del las Sosegadas. And she was *not* on the guest list.

Francesca felt her chest get tight with panic. Vale's ex-lover, princess or no, could *not* ruin this for her. She whirled away from the window. She had to do damage control. To make a big deal about the woman's appearance—as though she had been thoughtfully and graciously invited.

As though they were all the best of friends. So the press could not twist it into something that might cause a problem. So this woman could *not* interrupt her very necessary wedding.

In retrospect, this moment should have been Francesca's first clue that she did not wield *quite* the control she thought she did.

She reached for her mobile to call her assistant but didn't finish the move because she heard the door to the room squeak open. As she had been insistent that she wanted to be alone to have some private, *prayerful* contemplation before the ceremony, she assumed this interruption would be her father—who was still under the impression marrying Vale had been *his* idea, *his* boon, *his, his, his*.

Gritting her teeth, she took a breath and fixed the smile of servitude on her face and turned to face him. The last time, she promised herself, she'd ever have to pretend. She would get rid of him and then—

Except it wasn't her father. It was not anyone she knew. At least personally. She'd seen this man's face splashed across a dozen magazines and gossip sites. She had heard stories of him from *everyone* around her— except Vale, who was *very* careful to mention his wild, impetuous, illegitimate half brother as little as possible.

They looked so very much alike. Thick dark hair, broad shoulders, arrestingly handsome features and olive skin. They could have been twins, really, except for the eyes. Vale's were blue. This man's were brown.

And perhaps that *smile*. Which spoke of a wildness and danger that if Vale had, he kept hidden well under wraps.

"Ciao," he offered, very carefully closing the door behind him. Aristide wore an impeccable tuxedo that couldn't be all that much different than Vale's groom attire. And yet, where Vale would look ruthlessly styled, perfect from every angle just like her, Aristide Bonaparte somehow gave off the aura of casual insolence. His dark hair wasn't mussed but seemed to hint that a woman's fingers had been trailing through it not all that long ago. His posture was straight, his shoulders broad, and still he gave the impression of a man who could care less about what went on around him.

Because in his world, everything revolved around *him*.

It was strangely dizzying, all these suggestions that weren't the reality of the man who stood before her. For a moment, she forgot about her very pressing business of a princess crashing her wedding.

"Hello," Francesca replied carefully. When he said nothing, she remembered herself. Smiled. Lowered her gaze to unassuming timidity. "You are Aristide, are you not? Vale's brother."

"I am Valentino's half brother, yes."

He didn't offer anything else. Francesca tamped down her frustration—he was ruining her timetable. She needed to get *her* version of the Princess's arrival out before anyone else did. Still, she kept her smile in place and decided to treat this like a meeting. Smile. Shake hands. Ask questions. Feign interest and get to the bottom of why he was here. She held out her hand. "I am Francesca. It is so good to mee—"

He took her outstretched hand, but he did not shake it. He simply held it, turned it slightly to the right and then the left, as if to watch her jewelry sparkle in the light. Something about the move, the contact, the size of his hand made it somehow impossible to finish her sentence.

Slowly, he moved his gaze from her hand, and up to her eyes. The impact of all that swirling dark—knowing and arrogant, with a hint of humor she had definitely never seen in Vale—felt like a detonation.

"Yes, I am very well aware of who you are, *cara*."

His smile felt like some kind of lethal blow. Francesca could not understand why it should make her feel breathless and devastated.

But she had spent her life in such a state. So she kept her smile in place and waited patiently for him to explain his appearance. Even if her heart seemed to clatter around in her chest like it was no longer tethered. A strange sensation indeed.

"I am afraid there has been a change of plans today," he said at last, his low voice a sleek menace.

Francesca kept her sweet smile in place, her hand relaxed in his grip, her posture perfect. She was an expert at playing her role. Even as panic began to drum its familiar beat through her bloodstream. "Oh?" she said, as if she was interested in everything he had to say.

No one would change her plans. *No one.* She narrowly resisted curling her free fingers into a fist.

"You will be marrying me instead."

Francesca prided herself on being the kind of woman who could roll with the punches—after all she'd been dealt plenty of the literal kind. She held her mask up no matter the circumstances, but her mouth dropped open at that. "I'm sorry…what?" She jerked her hand away before she thought the action through to put a positive spin on it.

But why be positive to a man who was clearly *insane*.

"Vale has made a solid choice in such an upstanding character as yourself. So upstanding, I simply must have you for myself."

For himself? She shook her head, taking a step back away from him and then another. "That is *not* the plan, and…it's ludicrous." So ludicrous that… "Is this some kind of prank? I regret to inform you, a wedding day is *not* the day to try and pull one." She already had unwelcome royalty to deal with.

Aristide shrugged. "No prank. I am known for the ludicrous, of course. But you will be my bride, Francesca. We will leave at once and we will be married before the day is through. You can make that easy, of course."

She barked out a laugh. Not her usual dainty one either. She breathed in through her nose, reminding herself that she was *this* close to escape. She would not be thwarted now. "I don't understand what this is, but as *this* wedding is almost upon us, I think I shall see my plans and promises through." She smiled. "Thank you," she added.

But he did not look put in his place or swayed in any way. The curve of his mouth stayed arrogant and knowing. His eyes trailing over her like she was a possession he was determining the value of.

His possession.

It should disgust her, but she was too thrown off by all these unexpected things to really dissect the strange feeling that spiraled through her.

"You misunderstand me. You will either come with me to *our* wedding, or I will stop your wedding to Valentino in *other* ways, and from everything I've seen of you, *angioletta*, that would be a catastrophe. So, shall we go?"

Aristide Bonaparte had a few expectations of how this would go. The most likely reaction would be dramatics, of course, but everything he'd discovered about Francesca Campo in the past forty-eight hours since he'd decided she would be *his* bride, instead of his half brother's, pointed to a woman who did not do dramatics. Ever.

She was a bit of a tabloid favorite—for all the opposite reasons he was. Her father trotted her about from glittering event to posh dinner, creating an image of the perfect heiress. Full of goodness, warmth, and a heart of gold. Any man would be lucky to have her, and so it made the most sense that the great, honorable Valentino Bonparate would win her.

Aristide, on the other hand, was known as a *playboy* who cared for nothing and no one but his own pleasures and whims. No one would celebrate their union.

At first.

Aristide doubted he or Francesca were as bad or as good as the press made them out to be. The great thing about his plan was it didn't matter. The fact Vale was going to marry this woman only proved that even if she was not *privately* everything she made herself out to be, publicly she would be everything Aristide needed.

You could never have the kind of reputation your brother has built.

Aristide wanted to sneer at the memory of his detestable father's dismissive words—delivered via messenger, because that was the only way his father deigned to communicate with him these days. Aristide didn't mind living down to a low expectation—as long as he could take it even lower, but there was one man he *always* wanted to prove wrong.

So, he would.

Besides, it would be a fun little challenge to completely rebuild his public persona—as everyone said he couldn't—while feeling the satisfaction of embarrassing Vale, the betrayer.

A man had to find enjoyment where he could, and Aristide *always* found his.

Francesca had stopped backing away from him, stopped shaking her head. She was staring at him with wide eyes.

He would give all the stories and gossip about her one thing. She *was* beautiful, in an unearthly sort of way. Like she didn't quite belong in this world. But he did not think it was some *inner goodness* everyone else attributed it to. She was not a saint from a better world. Not an *angel*.

No, there was too much calculation going on behind those dark eyes. Because she didn't reach for her phone, and she didn't make a run for it as he'd half expected she might. No, she stood there. Regal and considering.

Instead of, say, screaming.

"How would you ruin my wedding to your brother?"

Interesting that the question was not *why*. But that was neither here nor there. "So many options, but I think the best is to wait for the priest to offer the crowd a chance to object, and to choose that moment to claim that you cannot marry my brother when you have been spending your nights with me."

Once again, the woman's mouth dropped open before she seemed to get ahold of herself. "What a ridiculous lie. Why would Vale believe that? Why would *anyone*? I've never even *met* you!"

Clearly, Francesca Campo did not know his brother

all that well. "It does not need to be true for Valentino to believe it of me. Regardless of anything he might feel about you, he's quite determined to believe the worst of me. Always. So, as you can see, it is in your best interest to come along." He held out his arm. He had planned and timed this perfectly, but he didn't have time for extensive conversations on the matter until he got her into his car.

"You want me to go with you," she said, very calmly. She even brought her hands in front of her and clasped them, as though she were conducting a meeting. "Marry you, instead of your brother, immediately?"

"Yes."

"And... You live on the island as well, yes?"

He very nearly frowned. He'd expected some...upset. Some tears, even if he knew she'd have to come with him after that threat. But this was all very...calm. "Yes." The island had been split nearly in two, between him and his brother. His estate was on the opposite side of the island, the *good* side, he liked to tell Valentino the rare moments they were in each other's presence.

Usually only at the Diamond Club they both belonged to—exclusively for the richest people in the world. Aristide smiled to himself. His brother still wasn't over the fact Aristide had gotten himself an invitation. And *loved* to appear when he knew Valentino would be there. Just to twist the knife.

"And after we were married, we would live here?" his future bride asked with clear eyes and a speculative expression.

"Indeed. Some even say *my* estate is much more livable than Valentino's mausoleum." He smiled at her.

She did not smile back.

"It is quite well known that you are…not selective, shall we say, with your romantic exploits. Why would you want to marry at all?"

"The years have weighed on me," he lied. Easily. "I want to rehabilitate myself, start a new leaf, and what better start than the perfect wife?" It was *told* that this woman was quite intelligent, but if she believed this story, clearly people were wrong.

Her expression didn't change. "Yes, stolen brides and threats are known to be a great start for a character change." Her delivery was so dry it nearly took him a moment to understand her true meaning.

He was tempted to laugh. "My, my, *cara*. Do I sense a flicker of a personality underneath all that polish?"

Her eyes cooled, but she didn't jump to the bait. "What about a contract?"

There was something downright *mercenary* about her. It was quite surprising, and Aristide didn't care one way or another if he *enjoyed* his chosen bride, but it would be nice to know she wasn't *quite* the wet blanket the press and his brother had painted her as. "I have drawn one up that is almost identical to the one you were to sign with my brother. With my name instead, of course."

"How did you have access to the contract we drew up?"

He shrugged. "Dastardly means, naturally."

She sighed as if she was vaguely irritated with him. A bit like his mother did when he was purposefully baiting her. "So, we will just go. Now? And be married…?"

she asked, still so unreadable, steady dark eyes study-ing him as though he were a complex math equation she would no doubt figure out if given the right tools.

It was unnerving, and not at all what he'd expected.

But this had always been where Aristide excelled. His name did not mean *the best* for nothing.

"Immediately," he supplied.

Yet again, he braced himself for some kind of reac-tion. Tears. Despair. Anger. Fear. Maybe even demands.

But this woman simply nodded a regal chin. "Very well."

This was not what he expected. He raised an eye-brow. "That easily?"

"You threatened to ruin this wedding either way, if you recall." Inexplicably she looked behind her, out the window that looked down over where guests were enter-ing. Then her gaze returned to him, dark and direct. "I know enough of your character to know you have ample means to accomplish this. Is capitulating to a threat *easy* or is it the intelligent course of action?"

No, she was not quite what anyone had made her out to be. *Fascinating.* "You didn't even try to get around it."

She waved this away as she walked over to her van-ity table and picked up a mobile and a small purse that matched the white of her bridal gown. She fixed him with a gaze that had a strange ribbon of unease move through him, like he was getting in over his head.

When that was as ludicrous as she accused this turn of events of being.

She lifted her chin. "I am determined to be married today, and the identity of the groom is rather immaterial if the contractual terms remain identical. You have just as much money as Vale, you have just as much land on this island. The two of you are basically interchange-able to me if the contract is indeed the same. I need a groom. I don't need a scandal."

He frowned at that. That was *his* line. It suited his purposes that she be this amenable, though he was baf-fled what the perfect, honorable Valentino was doing marrying a woman who felt her groom was *immaterial* and *interchangeable*.

"I assure you, nothing about my brother and I are the same."

She studied him, like she could see through his every thought. Ridiculous. "If you wish to think so, I won't argue with you."

"Excellent. I prefer a wife who doesn't argue."

Her expression went even more bland, sweet, *inno-cent*. "Of course," she said, and there was no reason not to believe she was exactly that unassuming.

He was surprised to find he did not believe the image she presented. At *all*.

But it did not matter. He would get what he wanted. Always.

CHAPTER TWO

ARISTIDE DID NOT *sneak* her away from Vale's estate, precisely. He just seemed to know where to go in the long, complex hallways where they ran into no people. Then out a side kind of servant entrance and into the bright sunny afternoon on the other side of the estate, opposite to where the wedding was taking place.

Francesca was very well aware she had options. She could have run to find Vale. She could have used her mobile to call for reinforcements. Maybe it would have created a bit of a scandal for the brothers to essentially fight over her, but she had little doubt she could still ensure a wedding to Vale by the end of the day.

Maybe, just maybe, if the Princess had not shown up, Francesca would have done just that, but something about the alluring, *interesting* beauty felt like the only true threat to Francesca's arrangement with Vale. Not just *today*, but the entire future of their marriage.

She couldn't risk Princess Carliz being a ghost that threatened her freedom. So she'd take this *ludicrous* course of action, as long as it got her what she wanted. The end result was all that mattered. Not how she got there.

As she'd noted, Aristide was not known for his long-term *relationships*. There would likely be scandal attached to him, but the kind of scandal she could no doubt weather if it kept her out of her father's orbit. Not the kind of scandal that would end her freedom if Vale truly *did* love Carliz and would end up leaving her for the beautiful princess.

Sometimes, you had to pick your poison based on what effects you could survive.

Aristide led her to a sleek sports car and opened the passenger door for her. She didn't hesitate to slide into her seat, to arrange herself gracefully, smoothing out the skirt of her dress as he moved into the driver's side.

"Will there be guests at our wedding? A photographer?" she asked as he pulled out of the long, winding drive.

They both pretended they didn't see a suited man— likely security—trying to wave them down.

"No. Our love could not wait for such accoutrement, naturally."

She wanted to laugh, but she kept her expression mild. Until the contract was signed, she had to play this very carefully. Aristide was not as…contained as Vale. He was known for whims and wildness, even if he wanted a reputation redo, and perhaps Francesca could hope to be more of herself in private once the ink was dry.

But the ink had to be dry first.

Besides, Aristide hit the gas pedal as though the very hounds of hell were on their heels and took the curves at a breakneck speed that had Francesca looking for *something* to grab on to. In the end, she could only brace herself against the door and hope she did not end up dying in a fiery crash in the wrong brother's car.

Now, *that* would be a story for the press.

She wanted to laugh again. What a dizzying and irresponsible way to travel.

Why did it feel like freedom?

None of this was what she'd planned, but then, what had ever gone according to her exact plans? She could make this one work. She *would* make this one work.

Aristide had a completely different reputation than Vale, but it was still one that might be enough of a threat to her father to keep him far away. And then there was the contract.

"Did you read the contract when you stole it to replicate it with your name?" she asked him, watching as the landscape passed by at dizzying speeds.

Aristide's gaze slid to her briefly, then back to the road, where he took another curve hard and sharp. "Naturally."

"So you know what will be required of you if you marry me?"

"Protection from your father—both in location and monetarily. An interesting choice of terms, *angioletta*."

The press had been calling her that since she'd been a little girl. She worked hard not to scowl. "I don't care for that nickname."

"But everyone loves to portray you as just that. A little angel."

"Then I suppose I should call you *piccolo diavolo*." She didn't wince, though she wanted to. She needed to hold her tongue. *Until the ink is dry.* It had been her motto to get to this day, and now it would be her mantra to get through this unexpected turn of events.

"Calling me a devil does not bother me in the least, but I would hesitate to characterize anything about me as *little*."

His smile was so self-satisfied it was nearly contagious. This was all nearly *funny*, really, but he took a hill too fast and her stomach flipped into her throat and then back down again.

She needed to focus on what he thought of the contract responsibilities, not finding his ridiculousness *amusing*. But she needed to find a smart way to negotiate. This might have been the easier course of action, but until the marriage certificate was signed and filed, this was perilous.

She had to behave as though every step was *imperative*.

They drove down the coastline of the island. She had not paid much attention to Vale's family beyond what he'd mentioned of it. He *never* mentioned Aristide if he could help it. And she had certainly never pressed. Especially after she'd had tea with Vale and his odious father.

It seemed best to be involved as little as possible in the Bonaparte soap opera, and she also knew enough not to step on toes.

She knew Vale and Aristide did not get along, did not agree on perhaps *anything*, and Vale considered Aristide an embarrassment. And an enemy, there on the other half of *his* island, *his* rightful inheritance—according to him.

For a moment, she felt a pang of guilt for leaving

Vale in the lurch. Perhaps she should have fought harder against his enemy.

But in the end, Vale was a rich, powerful man. He could withstand losing her. Besides, he had a princess there, no doubt just for him.

Francesca could not withstand losing her chance at freedom.

"I will need to look through the contract before we marry, of course," Francesca said. "Just to ensure it *is* the same."

"Naturally, though I can assure you I have no need to change anything. A perfect bride on paper, a good reputation, this is all I'm after. I will pay your father off and never allow him on the island."

She let out a careful breath. That was all that was needed. She could weather everything else if he did that alone. But…if Aristide was expecting *rehabilitation* as payment…

"Do you really think stealing your brother's bride is going to rehabilitate a terrible reputation you've spent your entire adult life exacerbating?"

"If *you*, *angioletta*, fell in love with a man such as me, enough to throw Vale aside and marry me, surely there must be some good in me."

"Ah, so we are meant to pretend we're in love, rather than the truth." She could do that. She'd been pretending her whole life. It was just strange that for the first time in so long, the pretense felt more like a new weight than the old one she was used to carrying.

"What would you prefer, considering you find the identity of your groom *immaterial*?"

"I didn't say I didn't prefer it. I'm just trying to understand the layout of this arrangement as I cannot believe that a man such as yourself believes much in monogamy. Respectability. Love."

"No, I do not believe in love, *cara*. But I cannot imagine a woman who considers her groom *immaterial* thinks much of it either."

"No. I don't." Love was a fairy tale for people who could afford one. Probably a *princess*. Perhaps with some years of security under her belt she might wish for such things, but for now, there was only escape.

"Relax, Francesca, we will give each other exactly what we need."

"And what is it you think I need?"

"Based on that contract and your lack of concern about the identity of your groom? I think you need escape. Any way you can get it. I think you want freedom, and I can give this to you easily. Happily, in fact, as your freedom harms me in no way at all."

"And what is it you need?" she asked, studying his profile as he drove recklessly. Like he had no cares, but if he wanted to become respectable, he would need to find a way to care about that.

"Simply the foundation on which to rebuild my reputation. Sainted wives are a great foundation."

What a depressing thought. She was so very tired of being other men's *foundations*. But that heavy cloud of *what have I gotten myself into* lifted as a large, sprawling, what could only be termed *castle* came into view beyond his profile.

"Welcome home, *angioletta*," he murmured.

Something like excitement fluttered through her at the sight. It was… It was… "It is certainly not a mauso-leum." Not that she thought Vale's estate was as grim as Aristide had been making it out to be, but there *was* a difference. Vale's was all stark, ancient, *ordered* beauty. Respectability seemed layered into every brick.

This was…chaos. Spirals and color. The ocean some-how more dramatic in the background because of the lack of order. Like it could win, any day, and all this… what have you would be swept away.

It was…thrilling.

"A masterpiece, isn't it?" he said, with no humility whatsoever. "Come. Let us promise to love one another for eternity."

Francesca's beauty was something else in the light of dusk and candlelight. She *looked* like an angel, stand-ing there across from him in the little chapel-like room. It was not a *religious* room, per se, but he was a man who liked the superficial beauty of the church without the heft of threats of punishment and hell.

He had built this estate, piece by piece, to whatever whim had struck him at the time. So it was only what *he* liked. Only what *he* cared to be surrounded by. He had learned early that to care what other people wanted never ended well for him.

So he drowned himself in his own wants and lived a much happier life than his brother, who lived as if con-stantly housed in a prison of the Bonaparte name.

Perhaps, on occasion, he purposefully chose what he knew Vale would hate. Like the naked mermaid weather vane undulating on top of one of the tall, twisting spires. Valentino would consider it crass, embarrassing, a black mark on the Bonaparte name.

Good.

Francesca had not displayed the reaction he had expected when they'd initially arrived. He'd expected that having been intended for his brother, she might share Vale's disgust for the chaos of it all.

Instead of vague disapproval, or poor attempts to hide it, she had looked up in *awe*. As though she quite enjoyed what she saw. Like she'd just been taken to a fairy-tale castle where dreams might come true.

This had pleased him. He'd enjoyed watching her take it all in. He'd enjoyed watching the way her smile softened her beautiful face, and *life* had sparkled in her dark eyes.

There was *something* of interest under that outer shell of perfection. Perhaps he was not sentencing himself to years of boredom if she could find some pleasure in the ridiculousness of his choices.

Then she had insisted upon poring over the marriage contract. She had read every word, every punctuation mark, *three* times. She had asked question after question until he'd felt as if they were in a boardroom and his eyes might cross from the banality of it all.

But he'd seen what was under her fastidiousness. A determination to get exactly what she wanted out of this union. To *ensure* it. So calculating and exacting. Admittedly, the world's perfect angel being a bit mercenary had been…arousing.

The current image of her, bathed in soft light,

wrapped in bridal white, while the officiant yammered on about love and duty, was not *less* arousing. Like there might be as many different fascinating facets to his bride as there were to the big, unwieldy diamond now on her finger.

A problem, because no doubt his Francesca was as virginal as they came—even if she wasn't everything the world thought she was. Wife or not, he didn't have any designs on preying on some sheltered innocent.

He preferred everyone know exactly what they were getting themselves into. He preferred having very careful lines that he did not allow anyone—himself included—to cross.

Of course, he would have to behave himself to begin to rehabilitate his reputation. There couldn't be even a whiff of an affair—and if there was anything he'd learned from his brother, it was that a man didn't have to act on his passions and whims for people to determine what might have happened with a beautiful and fascinating woman—the only kind Aristide preferred.

So Aristide would have to submit himself to *some* sort of celibacy to keep his lines intact. What a pity.

Perhaps he had not thought this plan fully through, but that had never been his strong suit. He was a man who acted and dealt with whatever consequences befell him. His brother had once accused him of only *ever* reacting, and perhaps in that one way Vale had been right.

Aristide felt there was nothing wrong with it. These were his consequences, and he would find a way around them. One way or another.

"I do," Francesca said very solemnly, bringing Aristide back to the ceremony at hand. He listened to the officiant recite the same promises he'd already outlined for Francesca. Then gave his own grave *I do*.

As the officiant announced them as married in front of precisely two witnesses—Aristide's assistant and his driver—Aristide allowed himself the satisfaction of knowing he'd done what he'd set out to do.

Stolen his brother's bride.

A coup indeed.

"You may kiss your bride, Signor Bonaparte."

Aristide had kissed many a woman in his day—and not *only* with the express purpose of talking them into bed. But he had never kissed *his* wife before. What a strange first to feel suddenly uncomfortable with.

But Aristide didn't *do* uncomfortable.

Francesca tipped her chin up, met him with that steady, dark gaze. She had taken this all in stride, with only a short moment or two of surprise back at Valentino's. He found he wanted to see that *true* reaction back on her face, instead of all these pretends she wore so effectively.

And Aristide did not know how to get through to this woman, but he knew how to get through to *women*.

He reached out, gripped her lifted chin between his thumb and forefinger, drawing her closer, while the remaining fingers brushed featherlight across her neck.

Her breath shuddered out, her eyes were wide on his. Not quite the prepossessed mercenary he'd seen before. Not the sweet, timid mask she wore so well—or some sign of her well-guarded virginity. No, there was something else entirely in that reaction.

That unease he'd first felt at Vale's was back, curling around deep inside him. A gut feeling that she might be more than he'd bargained for. A consequence, rather than the answer to his challenges.

Then she smiled, demure and sweet, and he *knew* she would be a problem.

A problem he was now contractually obligated to solve. But first, kiss. As had often happened in his life, he found himself struck with the urge to upend something. In this case, the serene, blank look on her face.

He had *meant* to remain fully hands off. A marriage in name only. Lines not crossed. And it would be that.

After this.

He lowered his mouth to hers, still holding her chin, pausing right there. Taking in the details of that beautiful face that he'd seen in print so many times, but never flesh and blood, never up close and personal.

The aristocratic nose, the heart-shaped face aiding in all the talk of *angels*. A little ring of hazel around the inner edge of wide eyes. The hint of gold in her left eye only.

And he waited, *waited* until he felt her breath hitch, just enough, to swoop in and finally close that minuscule distance between them. He wasn't sure what to expect, exactly, but that was half the fun of a kiss.

But he could not characterize this as *fun*, the gentle softness of her lips, the hesitant give of her body. The way she smelled of the wild oleander that permeated this island—like she belonged here when only his cursed bloodline truly belonged on this island of acrimony and pain.

It was a twist to the gut, a strange bolt of electricity, as though God himself was striking down this union. Devil to angel. *Cursed.*

He pulled back, not sure what…any of that was. He had kissed women before where the chemistry did not quite live up to what he preferred. He had kissed women perfectly pleasantly and blazed through passion often.

But he had never felt any of…that. Nor been left with this uneasy sort of…foreboding in response to a simple kiss.

She looked up at him, and he could not *read* her, there hidden behind whatever masks she wore.

He had thought this would be so straightforward. Steal Valentino's boring, sainted bride. Well, stealing Vale's toys had never gone quite according to plan, so why would he think it different now?

He dropped her chin. Smiled just as blandly as she and waited for the officiant to dismiss them. Once he did, Aristide took her by the arm and led her out of the room.

"Come, I will show you to your suite. Once the dust has settled over at Valentino's, we shall have your things brought over here. In the meantime, I am sure we can supply you with whatever you need."

"Dust." She blew out a breath. "I suppose I should feel some guilt for that."

"But you don't?"

"Vale will survive," she said with a firm nod. "And now, so will I."

"So dramatic, *angioletta.*"

She did not respond to that. Just marched on next to

him as he led her through the maze of hallways, curving stairwells. This place made no real architectural sense, which was why Aristide loved it. The island might be cursed, but this was his antidote.

This was where he could be whatever he damn well pleased, without concern about what anyone else thought or needed. A hard-won lesson he now embodied full throttle.

Much like the architecture, the woman next to him didn't make the sense he thought she had either. But they had time yet. He would puzzle her out. She was just a person like any other. He would understand, and all would be as he wanted it to be.

Always.

He led her to what would be her suite of rooms. For appearances, they connected to his own, but there was plenty of space for the two of them to exist as apart as they wished as the years wore on.

He tried not to think in *years*.

He opened the door to the main part of the suite. "Through here, you will find your bedroom and private bath. You will—"

But it was clear she wasn't listening to him. She certainly wasn't following him to the other rooms. She walked straight to the door that led out to the balcony that looked down over the beach. She didn't stop until she reached the edge, curling her hands around the railing and looking down at the crashing waves.

He followed her out into the balmy night. Darkness had fallen, but the lights of his estate—always bright and blazing *at* his brother—illuminated her gaze as it tracked across the coastline, the glittering moon and stars. Her expression began to soften, her full lips slowly curving into a smile. A *real* smile that threatened to outshine the moon itself.

Then she turned to him, a brightness in her that was all new. All…alarming.

"Might I have some champagne? Perhaps some cake. I feel like celebrating." And she *looked* like a celebration. She couldn't seem to keep the grin off her face. Her eyes were sparkling and a joyous energy pumped from her.

"Celebrating your marriage to a stranger?"

"I have lived under the thumb of my father for twenty-four years. And now I am finally free. *That* is cause for celebration. Whatever the means, whatever the cost, I am finally free." She shook her head vaguely, as if she couldn't quite believe it, and looked back out at the ocean.

"You do realize that some become adults and obtain jobs and leave their parents' thumbs with no dramatic marriages required?"

She stiffened, some of that unbridled joy leaving her face. Everything in her expression smoothed out, until she looked like…anyone. There was nothing special about this woman if he believed this facade she could shroud herself with.

But that she could was fascinating enough.

"I had not considered that." She clasped those hands so tight it pointed at something more than the lifeless words. "I was raised to believe marriage was my only option, of course, so that is the option I took." She smiled blandly up at him, her eyes devoid of anything.

But what she said was not true. It wasn't that he could read the lie on her. It was more her insistence that the contractual terms protect her from her father, combined with this freedom she wanted to celebrate, that had him wondering what went on at the Campo estate in Rome.

"Perhaps we could set aside these pretends and speak the truth. After all, we are husband and wife." And because he could not *quite* resist being himself, he grinned. "We must share all kinds of things now."

CHAPTER THREE

FRANCESCA REMINDED HERSELF that this was all part of the plan. That she had gotten exactly what she wanted, even if the groom was different. Even if he now spoke of *truths* and...*sharing* things.

Perhaps it was not as sturdy as the agreement she and Vale had made, but she had a contract. A signed contract. A signed marriage license. She was free. She was safe.

What did truths matter? Perhaps this was *better*. Even if Aristide wanted to use her reputation to salvage his own, she couldn't make his *worse*. There wasn't nearly as much pressure here as there would have been as Vale's wife, and there wouldn't be constant comparisons to one very beautiful and interesting princess.

There *would* be speculation, raised eyebrows, and perhaps concern. For her. But she did not have to be as perfect as she'd always been—because she would always look better than Aristide.

Besides, truths laced with omissions were not *lies*. They were self-protection. So she gave him a watercolor version of the truth.

"You have a rather awful father of your own, based on

everything I've experienced with Vale. Surely you can imagine how a rich and powerful man might keep his daughter exactly where he wants her. A job? Who would hire me knowing Bertini Campo would sweep in and make their lives hell if they did? Perhaps I should have run away. With what? Stolen money? That he would track down, easily enough. Nothing? He also would have tracked me down, or the press would have. Believe me, I tried every means of escape I could, but they were all thwarted. Except the one thing he wanted for me. All I had to do was ensure *I* was in charge of the groom and make him think it was his idea."

"Won't he be upset with this turn of events as you were, in fact, not in charge of the groom?"

Francesca smiled sweetly. "You are a Bonaparte, are you not? The contract is the same. My father still gets everything he wants. This will keep him happy and far away." She refused to think otherwise. "Surely you have some supply of alcohol and sweets in this castle of debauchery? I would like to celebrate," she said. She wanted to get drunk. She wanted to eat an entire cake. All things she'd never been allowed to do.

She was *free*, and she damn well wanted to celebrate getting everything she'd planned.

"I prefer other kinds of debauchery, *angioletta*."

She might be virginal, but she had heard more than her fair share of sexual innuendo in the course of growing up. She understood his meaning, all too well. Though it left a strange trail of warmth through her, not the usual nausea.

Her father never minded his oily friends *saying* inappropriate things, *looking* at her in inappropriate ways. He had, in fact, encouraged it. As long as no one got handsy. Her precious virginity was a selling point in the great amassing of *more*, but that didn't mean he'd protect her from being harassed in other ways.

No doubt Aristide, famous for his trail of women, would expect his own version of *more*. She hadn't… thought that part of the groom switch through, had she?

Well, she'd just keep brazening through these unexpected detours. As she always had before.

"Vale and I had an agreement when it came to…sharing things," she said quite forcefully.

Aristide raised a dark, aristocratic eyebrow. "Please tell me how you planned to share my brother's bed," he said, so dryly she might have cracked a smile if she was not so uncomfortable. "I can think of nothing I'd like to hear more about."

"Your sarcasm is not quite the weapon you think it is."

"And your reputation is not quite the one *you* think it is."

"You stole me for my reputation."

"Yes. I did. Though *stole* feels a *bit* dramatic, don't you think?" He held up a hand, a kind of "hold that thought" gesture, and then he disappeared inside. He was only gone a few moments before he returned with a bottle of champagne in a bucket of ice, and two glasses. He placed them on a small patio table in the corner. Then went about the process of opening the bottle—all dramatic movements capped by the popping of the cork. It made her jump.

She reminded herself to relax. She had gotten away from the hell of her childhood. Maybe this wouldn't be heaven, but it would be *better*.

Aristide poured two flutes of champagne. She had meant champagne for *herself*. She had meant celebrating *alone*. Still, she accepted the glass when he handed it to her and did not invite him to leave.

Much as she kind of wanted to.

He held up his glass. "To a mutually beneficial union."

Mutually being the operative word, she thought to herself before clinking her glass to his. She took a long, deep drink, trying to let the celebratory bubbles ease some of the coils of anxiety inside of her.

She was so happy to be free, and she wanted that to be enough, but this man across from her was making things…complicated.

He studied her with dark eyes as he sipped his champagne at half the pace of her. When he finally spoke, it was probably the most serious she'd yet to hear him. "There are no photographers here, Francesca. No businessmen I make deals with, gossips who spread stories about me. My staff is loyal and know their worth here is more than any story they could sell. Here, in *my* castle, it is simply you and me."

How she wanted that to be true. To simply be *her*. For once. For *once*. To follow her own whims, her own desires. It was hard to believe she'd actually get that, but…here was a man who did that. All the time. No matter the backlash.

Perhaps…perhaps she could learn something from

him. She lifted her glass, drained it and held it out for him to refill.

He obliged, but not without commentary.

"There is no rush."

"I think I'd like to get very drunk. I've never been drunk."

"Never?"

She shook her head. "Never been allowed even a full glass of champagne. Or more than one piece of cake on any given day. There was a woman employed by my father whose entire job it was to count my calories once I reached fifteen." She likely shouldn't have told him that, but she was free.

Free.

She could tell all the truths about her upbringing as she liked. She wouldn't go public with them, of course, but she didn't have to hide them from her *husband*.

She wanted to laugh at the absolute ridiculousness of that word, of this situation.

"What other *never*s are you looking to rid yourself of?" Aristide asked as he refilled her now drained glass.

She immediately took a sip from it. She liked the frothiness of it. The way it all seemed to go immediately to her head and make her feel less tethered to *everything* that weighed her down. She hadn't eaten today—too nervous, too determined to see everything through—so that likely added to the effect of it all. She could really use that whole cake right about now, but she decided to consider his question instead as she sipped from her glass.

She studied him. Maybe it was the alcohol. Maybe it was being in the desperate situation she found herself.

She knew better than to show her vulnerable underbelly, so she started with the superficial.

"I want to learn how to bake."

He waved it away as though it were nothing. "Easily done. I'll set you up with Maurizio first thing in the morning. He is world-renowned in the kitchen, and if he cannot teach you what you wish to know, he will find someone who does."

She blinked. She hadn't thought so far ahead as to actually…getting the things she'd always wanted. She had only wanted the possibility. She had only wanted the space to breathe. To be…safe.

But learning to bake was *easily* done, according to Aristide. She swallowed against the emotion rising in her throat.

"I want to sleep in. I've never had a pet. I always wanted a dog. Something big and ridiculous. The more hair, the less brains, the better." It was all too…much. She felt like crying suddenly. Just collapsing into a heap and sobbing her heart out.

But she would never do that in front of him. Or anyone else, for that matter. Champagne or no.

So she just kept listing things. "And…never, *ever* see another piece of gym equipment."

"I don't mind a good workout now and then, so of course I have a gym on the property, but you may avoid it all you wish. *I* prefer to get my physical exertion out elsewhere anyhow."

Another innuendo. She could let it go. Smile and nod like she usually did before extricating herself from an uncomfortable situation. But he was just so *casual* about the whole thing. He wasn't watching for her reaction. He wasn't playing some weird power game. She thought these lazy little comments were just…the kind of thing he was so used to saying he didn't even consider the true meaning.

Perhaps it was that realization. Perhaps it was the champagne. Perhaps it was this strange turn of events and a break with reality, but she looked him right in the eye and said her next sentence very, very clearly.

"I do *not* want to sleep with you." Which brought strange images to mind. Like that kiss back in the unique and beautiful room they'd been married in. The way his hand had felt on her face, the warmth that had pooled inside her, lower than it should. That strange shuddering thing that cascaded through her.

She had kissed—if you could even call it that—Vale once or twice for the demure photo op and there had never been any of *that*.

But Aristide did not get all puffed up and angry. He only smiled. "I didn't ask."

"I may be a virgin, but it is not in my experience that men do a lot of *asking*."

Something changed in his gaze just then. All that lazy indulgence sharpening ever so slightly, but the smile did not falter. "I'm a great believer in consent. And begging, naturally."

Begging. Her frank and brief discussion with Vale on the matter of marital relations when they'd been drawing up their contract had definitely not discussed consent or *begging*.

Francesca had no smart comeback, no quick quip.

So she simply stood there, and finished off yet another glass of champagne. All while Aristide stood—a good distance away on the balcony—*watching* her.

When he finally finished his one glass, he set it down on the table. And moved over to her. She held her breath, wondering if he'd touch her face again. Wondering if… something was about to happen. Her heart clamored in her chest, but she did not back away. And it wasn't her usual obedient mask that kept her rooted to the spot.

She didn't *want* to back away from the height and breadth of him, the heat of him.

What did that mean?

But he didn't touch her. "You are a fascinating creature, *angioletta*. Perhaps this entire endeavor will be more fun than I originally planned."

She didn't know what she was having. Not fun, per se. But this was…different. Liberating, maybe. Fun sounded…fun, though. "I don't think I've ever had any fun."

"Well, then we shall start tomorrow."

Aristide did not sleep well, but he did not allow himself to dwell on the *why*s.

He was an expert at denial.

He did not dwell on the way Francesca had smiled, or the look on her face when she spoke of some *woman*, hired by her father, counting her calories. Or how seriously she'd told him men did not do a lot of asking.

Her experiences up to this moment were immaterial. Whatever had happened before had no bearing on now.

He had a plan to enact.

This first week as husband and wife would be fairly quiet. To give the illusion of a cozy honeymoon at home. Then they would begin the real campaign. Events. Charity. And most of all convincing the entire world they were desperately in love.

What better story could there be than a debased playboy turning his life around for a perfect angel? Once he convinced them of it, everyone would *love* the story. Alone, he could never outshine Vale's perceived goodness, but with Francesca by his side?

He would have everything. And his father could go to hell.

Cheered by that thought, he went about preparing their morning. She'd said she wished to sleep in, so he had the staff prepare a brunch rather than a breakfast, to be set up outside once there were stirrings from Francesca's quarters.

When he was informed Francesca would arrive shortly, he made his way to the outdoor setup. It was already warm and sunny. Aristide had always loved the heat and shine of summer. The perfect backdrop for excess, he liked to think.

When his bride arrived on the sprawling, ornate patio, she was dressed in something bright and flowy— a swimsuit cover-up, if he had to guess by the brevity of the skirt. She looked around—at the statues of mythical creatures that lined the stairs leading down to the beach, the waves, the sun in the distance, the table of food.

But not at him.

"Good morning," she greeted, studying the layout of food quite seriously.

"Good morning, my wife. Join me for brunch."

She did not sit down. "Vera said the best time for a swim would be now," she said, speaking of the staff member he'd assigned to take care of Francesca.

"She is right, but you should eat something first after your first night of champagne debauchery."

"Vera supplied aspirin."

"Which you shouldn't have on an empty stomach. Sit. Eat."

She eyed the table with a mix of avarice and distrust. "How could two people possibly eat all this?"

"Two people who aren't counting calories but are instead enjoying their honeymoon, *angioletta*."

Still, she did not meet his gaze. She settled herself into the seat across from him, and sat there, looking around like she couldn't possibly know where to begin.

So he decided to aid her. He got up and took her plate from its spot in front of her and then began to pile it up with buttered bread with jam, a *sfogliatelle*, an assortment of cheeses and figs, wedges of caprese cake and a spinach frittata. He poured her both juice and coffee and placed it all in front of her before returning to his seat.

"If I eat all of this before I swim, I fear I will simply sink."

Aristide shrugged. "Eat what you wish. Take a swim break and return. We are on our honeymoon, *cara*, we may laze about however we wish."

She inhaled through her nose, then gave a little nod like she was accepting orders to march into battle. She lifted her silverware, and only hesitated a moment before she spoke again.

"Have you heard…" She trailed off, placing a bite of frittata in her mouth, but he knew what she had wanted to ask even if she did not finish.

"You have access to all the same news outlets as I do, Francesca. If you wish to know what befell your jilted groom, you can look it up yourself."

"Yes, but you're his family. I thought perhaps you might know…"

"Trust that if it involves my 'family' I do not know any more than the next person. This is by design—theirs, and I have no need to change it."

"Don't you care what damage you might have done?"

"Damage?" Aristide snorted out a laugh. "Did I interrupt your grand love match, Francesca? I know I did not, because I know my brother. For all the ways he does not make sense to me, I'm pretty sure you both knew you were making a business deal. Nothing more. Therefore, whatever *damage* results, is something he'll no doubt slither his way out of as he always does."

She shook her head, pondering the pastry on her plate. Finally, *finally*, she lifted her gaze to his. All dark eyes. Still unreadable, but there was something soft in her expression.

He didn't care for it one bit.

"Why do you and Vale hate each other so much?" she asked. Gently enough to poke at his temper.

"Surely my brother made sure to paint me the dastardly villain in all his stories of me."

"He went through great effort to never discuss you at all."

Aristide scowled at that. It shouldn't *surprise* him,

and yet it felt like age-old dagger lodged into his back. "It is all very complicated, and very simple. He *thinks* I betrayed him with the truth. I *know* he betrayed me with his reaction to it." Aristide studied the mug of coffee, then set it aside as his stomach curled into a hard knot that often accompanied thinking too much of what had happened between him and Vale. "Perhaps we are both right."

"How did he betray you?"

Aristide considered the truth, and the lie he liked to trot out. He didn't mind the lie, liked playing it up for the right audience, but for some odd reason it felt wrong to lie to Francesca's interested gaze.

"We were quite close growing up, when he thought I was the lowly housekeeper's son and not his competition. When I discovered the identity of my father and informed him we were not just friends but brothers, I rather thought our connection was the only good thing to come out of something so terrible. He did not agree."

"That doesn't make much sense. Why would it matter whether you were related or not? You had no say in your existence."

Aristide shrugged, plucking a piece of cheese off his plate and studying it. Instead of taking a bite, he set it back down, not sure why he couldn't stomach the thought.

"It did not make much sense to me then, no. Part of the problem, I suppose. But as we have grown it has become clear that it was fine enough to be my friend when he thought me beneath him, but to think we might be the same made such a relationship difficult for his precious ego."

"Perhaps you are missing some piece to the story."

He met her gaze across the table. "I did not think you were in love with my brother."

She didn't bristle. She rolled her eyes, which for some reason eased some of the tension inside of him. "I'm not. But he was nothing but kind to me. And so have you been, so far. Aside from the whole stealing me away, I suppose. Not that I put up a true fight."

"I have never been accused of being *kind*, Francesca."

She gestured at the table. "But you have been."

"If supplying you with food on our honeymoon is a kindness, it will be quite easy to convince you I am the kindest man alive from here on out."

"Well, that would certainly help in redeeming your reputation. As would supplying me with a swimsuit with *any* modesty at all."

"If the clothes supplied are not the right fit—"

"It is not the *size* that is the issue, and as much as I have always been curious about skinny-dipping, it would not be…"

She had clearly not meant to say that, as she trailed off and blinked. Immediately snapping her mouth shut and looking vaguely embarrassed.

He liked that this woman of so many facets might have been comfortable enough to let a truth slip out without thinking it through.

"It is a private beach, *angioletta*. You may swim in as much or as little covering as you wish. Be my guest."

"Honestly, Aristide. If I should do *any* skinny-dipping, it would not be with *you* in attendance."

He liked the way she said his name. All haughty and clipped, like a scolding schoolteacher. Even as her cheeks turned a pretty shade of pink.

He grinned at her. "Ah. Pity."

She shook her head, but there was a curve of amusement to her lush mouth as she stood. "I am going to swim," she announced grandly, like she was waiting for him to argue with her. When he didn't, she started to walk toward the stairs that led down to the beach. She looked back over her shoulder at him. Once. "You may join me, but I am *not* taking off my bathing suit," she stated—not that he'd asked. But she was smiling, like it was a joke.

The same feeling from the chapel swept over him. This swirling, soaring feeling that could only mean bad things were on the way. It could only be *dread*, even if it ribboned with a lightness that seemed created by her and her alone.

Aristide tracked her progress to the beach. He considered joining her, as he quite enjoyed a morning swim in the surf himself, but then she drew the cover-up off her.

There was no doubt she was beautiful. The wedding gown she'd worn yesterday had not *hidden* her body, per se. He'd been able to see the outline of her curves, the slender slope of her elegant shoulders, the flare of her hips. There were no surprises in the swimsuit—which was hardly *immodest*. Yes, it was two pieces, but the swath of olive skin visible between the dark fabric was hardly obscene.

It was that something in her expression had changed as she stepped into the calm, waving surf. All that calculation, all that *fake*, washed away. It was the joy he'd seen last night on her face when she spoke of freedom, but now it seemed deeper, as she stood out there on her own in the water.

It was something about the *glow* of her. Like that dress had made her a statue, and this was the soul beneath it. She walked deeper and deeper in, turning to face him.

Her smile was like the sun itself. And then she flung herself backward and disappeared beneath the surface, only to appear again, hair wet and flowing behind her, reminding him of the foolish mermaid that he would see atop the spire behind him if he turned to look.

But he did not. Nor did he follow his initial thought to go down to the beach and swim with her. No, if he was determined to keep his hands off his virginal wife— and he *was*—it would be best if he stayed right where he was.

Someone cleared their throat behind him. It was some effort to take his gaze off Francesca as she dove and resurfaced over and over again. When he did finally turn, one of his staff members stood there with an envelope.

Aristide did not smirk, though he wanted to. Ah, finally, a response to his actions. Something to focus on besides his surprising new wife. But when he took the envelope and opened it, it was not his brother's stationery or harsh penmanship as he'd expected.

It was a short and to-the-point missive from father dearest.

You will come to my estate and discuss this at once.

Aristide crumpled up the piece of paper, wished for a fire so he could dramatically toss it in. He didn't care for the fact he'd been so certain he'd receive *something* from Valentino. Some reaction. Some…explosion. Something that might actually afford them the chance to clash.

It grated that he'd not considered his father might *also* have a response.

"Ignore it," Aristide told his messenger. "Ignore everything from Signor Bonaparte. I have made it clear to him I have nothing to say unless he can be bothered to show his face here." And that was one thing Milo Bonaparte refused to do. So it was easy to be as no-contact with his father as he liked at any given time.

Besides, as much as he was turning his reputation around to spite his father, that was not the attention he *really* wanted. He had long since given up on Milo Bonaparte, but there was another Bonaparte he couldn't quite seem to leave be.

Before Luca could fully withdraw, Aristide held up a hand. "Wait. Has anyone from Vale's estate brought over Francesca's things?"

"Not yet."

"Send a missive, just like this one but on my own stationery. Short and to the point, requesting Francesca's things be returned to her before the end of the day." If there was anything that might get under Valentino's steel armor, it would be something that *appeared* to be from their father but was from him instead.

Aristide smiled to himself and went back to watching his bride swim.

CHAPTER FOUR

FRANCESCA HAD ALWAYS loved to swim, but like all the things she'd loved that she'd managed to get her father's approval on, it had come with strings.

She couldn't just *play* in the water. She'd had to train like an Olympic swimmer, no matter that competition was *beneath* a woman of her important standing. Laps and correct form and instructors watching her every move. Timing her. Urging her to do better and be better. All for…nothing, really. She'd never understood it, but she'd borne it to get the thing she wanted.

But this was *more*. Here, she simply allowed herself to…play. Like a child. And the simplicity of it, the joy of it, caused tears to form in her eyes. And since she was essentially alone, she let them fall, then be washed away to sea.

She knew Aristide watched her, though she did not know why, but he was not close enough to see tears track down her face. He would not be able to tell them from the droplets of water. So she just let herself *feel*. Cry. Fall into the surf and pretend to drown, only to claw her way back up again and live.

Live.

It was like a baptism. A new life. Hope and joy. So big and bright she was almost afraid to believe it was true.

But the week went on just like that. All the things she'd packed for her new life as Vale's wife had appeared the second day, and other than some dark mutterings from Aristide about his brother, there seemed to be no real fallout from being *stolen away*. She hadn't heard from her father, from Vale angry with her, from anyone. There were stories, of course, but they all seemed to focus on Aristide and why he might have done such a thing.

She slept in, swam every morning—usually as Aristide watched from a distance. She ate luxurious meals, not at all concerned about calories or fat content, and spoke with her husband about anything and everything.

It was a struggle, though not a painful or unwanted one. Just… She had always been a quick study of people. Learned how to maneuver them to whatever suited the moment. It had been necessary when living under her father's iron fist.

But even with days under her belt, she did not know how to handle Aristide. He was an enigma. Not quite matching his reputation—which didn't surprise her as she knew she didn't match hers. But she couldn't quite figure out what the disparity was.

He acted as though nothing bothered him, just as his reputation suggested. He made lazy innuendos, but never pressed. Never *asked*. He was the epitome of respectability and kindness underneath that facade of reprobate.

It was the kindness, she supposed, that she allowed

herself to trust—slowly. Because she knew that kindness could not be *truly* faked. Meanness or true motives had always shown through. She knew he was kind to her not because he *cared* in any way, but because there was no reason to be *unkind* in these moments.

And she had precious little of that in her life.

Slowly, very slowly, she allowed herself to be…herself, instead of the outer shell her father had crafted. Always testing the waters, always careful not to show too much too quickly. But Aristide never seemed surprised or horrified by who she really was or what she really wanted.

She supposed this was one of the positives to marrying a man who, allegedly, had no morals or concerns.

Maurizio taught her how to bake. They'd started simple. Cookies. A cake. It was exhilarating, creating something delicious, though not always pretty, from simple ingredients.

"I did this one all on my own," she announced, perhaps more excited than she had a right to be over something as simple and humble as her *very* rustic *schiacciata alla fiorentina*. It was their fourth night, and Aristide sat out on the porch they often retired to with a drink. She brought out her cake with perhaps too much fanfare, but Aristide had yet to make her feel foolish for enthusiasm.

She sat the pan down on the table, cut a piece and placed it on a waiting plate. She walked over and took the seat next to him. She didn't know what possessed her, but she used the fork to section of a piece and then held it out to him.

"You get the first bite."

His mouth quirked up, all charming amusement. But he dutifully leaned forward and took the bite she offered. Their gazes held as he took the fork into his mouth.

It was like a jolt of electricity, a reminder of the way her body had reacted on their wedding day, except this time they weren't touching. And still that buzz of electricity moved over her skin, tightening and tingling all the way down deep into her core.

Francesca had no real experience with desire. She wasn't even sure she would have recognized the disorienting swirling if she hadn't read *some* romance novels—hidden from her father, of course.

But this felt like all of those descriptors. Wild and untamable. Alluring *and* alarming. Until she realized he'd taken the bite, so there was no reason to still be holding the fork up.

She dropped it to the plate like it had scorched her, when the only thing that had was this strange new heat he created inside of her.

"A feat, *angioletta*," he offered, and if she was not mistaken his voice was more gruff than usual. "I shall have two pieces."

She wanted to *giggle*, which was the most ridiculous thing. But it gave her an excuse to move. To serve him said two pieces, and then she went ahead and took two for herself. She settled into her chair, trying to resist the urge to study him as he ate.

It was such a strange thing, having spent some time with Vale, who had been…not harsh, exactly. But very… contained. There had been a stillness about him. A stillness she had recognized as the one she tried to project to the world around her.

Aristides was all energy. All action. He had this outer appearance of laziness, but there was such movement in him. Such...*reaction*, and it created this reaction in her too.

And not just that sparkling heat, but something else. He...sparkled, really. In conversation, in dinners where there were just the two of them. Even in silences such as now as he ate her cake. *Two* pieces.

He made her feel...

Well, she supposed that was it. Here in this strange world of his castle on his side of the island, she was just allowed to *be her*, for the first time *ever*. And there were a cascade of feelings that came from simply that.

Perhaps Aristide did not really *care* about her, nor did she expect him to. Perhaps he was wild in his personal life, reckless in business—though thus far it had only worked out for him. But he had never once been cruel to her or any of his staff. He had never once pressed her about *begging*, though she oftentimes felt his gaze hot and intent, like a brand itself.

It was like discovering a...friend.

"All those books you requested should be here tomorrow," he said over dinner the following night as the week came to a close.

Because he'd encouraged her to order practically a *library* full of books after she'd mentioned the types of fiction her father had never let her read—one of the few things she'd been able to successfully sneak under his nose, but not enough to truly satisfy her.

"Wonderful, but I suppose next week won't be quite as leisurely with lots of reading time."

"No, we must do some travel. Emerge from our love cocoon."

Francesca wrinkled her nose. "What a hideous term."

He chuckled. "And yet, this is what the stories I so very carefully plant will say. Never fear, it will not be all balls and dinners. You will have reading and swimming and baking time and whatever else here and there as time allows. You are not to be treated as a prisoner just yet."

She watched as he ate his dinner. Every move was languid, as if he had no care in the world. But he had plans, and no matter how different they might be, he surely had things he hadn't done because of who he was.

"What about you?"

"What *about* me?"

"Is there anything you've always wanted or wanted to do that you haven't been able to?" She sipped the wine, still even after nearly a week of this amazed that she could have as much or as little as she liked. She wanted to somehow offer Aristide the same.

Perhaps even some of that *same* reaction she felt from him.

Aristide raised those acrobatic eyebrows of his at her across the candlelit table. "What gives you the impression I have ever been under anyone's thumb?"

Francesca rolled her eyes, then took a moment to revel in the freedom of letting her face do whatever she pleased. "Surely there was something you haven't been able to do that appeals to you. Hot-air balloon rides?

Climbing Mount Everest? One of those dreadful races where you spend days going from terrible climate to terrible climate on foot? An African safari?"

"I assure you, Francesca, if I have wanted to do it, I have done it."

"Except rebuild your reputation." Which she could definitely do for him. She could be an *expert* at that. Maybe this entire week had been a ruse to gain her loyalty. But that thought did not bother her. It was simply a ruse that worked, if so.

"Precisely. And on that note, the real work must begin. Up first, we will attend Ludovica Gallo's ball in Rome."

She was tempted to make another face, and then, reminded herself she could make whatever faces she liked. She stuck her tongue out at the invitation Aristide slid her way.

He chuckled. "My sentiments exactly. Signora Gallo is a mean old beast, but she wields a lot of power among the gossips of our world. We must go to her ball and convince her we're madly in love."

"She always tells me I am too skinny. I think it is the only flaw she can find with me. It will likely be quite exciting for her to believe I could do something so foolish as to fall madly in love with you."

"Excellent. We want attention. Maybe even speculation to start, but over the course of the next few months we will build the image of the perfect couple. You have reformed me with your love and so on."

Love. He brought that word up a lot for someone who didn't believe in it, but she supposed that was the angle.

The fairy tale. The sainted good girl reforming the careless rake.

But *love*, or whatever went on between any man and woman that got the whispers going, would require more than going to balls on each other's arm. It would need more than their ability to have a pleasant conversation with one another. It would require…something more.

She did not think Vale had been gallivanting around with Princess Carliz behind her back, but he didn't *need* to, because people liked to whisper about the way they *looked* at each other, the way they couldn't be in the same room together. A chemistry *everyone* could feel, regardless of whether Vale and Carliz had acted on it at all. People were drawn to the *drama* of it all.

When it came to Aristide and Francesca, well, she supposed he *did* watch her, with intent eyes, any time they were together. And she might not know a *thing* about being kissed, but even knowing next to nothing about the real person inside of Aristide's many masks, she had been affected by their lone kiss at the altar.

Maybe it was foolish to think there was any kind of *attraction* in a kiss, in a look over a bite of cake. Maybe he was acting, and it was all about his plans.

But she didn't think so. Because he kept a very careful distance, even with his ever-present innuendos flung her way. And while she wasn't sure how she felt about closing that distance he kept, they would need to if his plan was going to work.

"You know, to convince other people we're in love, we'll have to exist in the same orbit," she said.

"Are we not doing exactly that right now?"

"Every meal you sit an almost entire length of table away from me. At the ball, we will be on each other's arm. We will have to sit next to one another. Likely we'll have to dance together. I have seen the pictures of many a model, actress, socialite et cetera draped across your arm. There is not an entire expanse of space between you and them when you walk into a ballroom."

"Is this not the respectability we are in search of? I was not under the impression that saints went about groping one another in public."

It was such a ridiculous image, she laughed in spite of herself. "Love and respectability are two different things entirely. We must accomplish the image of both." Deciding to take matters into her own hands now that she had an objective, she stood. She dragged her chair down the length of the table and set it next to his before retaking her seat.

Aristide raised an eyebrow at her. "And what exactly will sitting elbow to elbow this evening for our meal do?"

"It's called practice, Aristide. One must practice to get good at anything. We will need some work at portraying the image of a couple in love. And the lessons must begin now if we are meant to be successful at Signora Gallo's."

"I have never been much of a believer in lessons, practice, or anything else that sounded like *work*."

She made a considering noise, because that could hardly be true when he'd amassed his own fortune independent of his father's, but she was beginning to figure him out. He was more complicated than most—she'd certainly never spent more than a day or two puzzling out a member of the opposite sex—but there were telltale signs anyone gave off. When they were being serious, when they were putting up a mask, pretending to be what everyone else saw.

She would know. And she would maneuver him accordingly until she fully understood who he was underneath all that.

So she did not argue with him, even though she knew he had not spoken a full truth. "Unfortunately, if your plan is to work, you will have to put forth an effort in all those things. You married me for a reason, did you not? Trust that while my father controlled every aspect of my being that he could, *I* quickly learned how to make everyone including him think exactly what I wanted them to think about me. We can do the same for you, but you will have to take instruction. And you will have to practice."

"I do not care for these stories of your father's overbearing control." He said it in the same dark way he often talked about his own father. Something fluttered in her chest, but she ignored it.

It had never mattered what anyone else thought of her father or his behavior. It only mattered that she was free of it now. "Join the club. He will likely be there. A ball in Rome? He won't miss it." She tried not to dwell on that, on seeing him again, on all the pretend that lay in front of her after this week of fantasy life. Just her. Just the ocean. Just her husband she didn't fully know enjoying a cake she'd made.

Instead, she focused on her mission. She was free

now, so what did her father matter? He could not take her home after and keep food from her, use his fists on her, rage and throw things at her.

No. That was over. And in order to ensure it, she had to make sure Aristide knew how to pretend they were in love for everyone to see.

"Now, when we are sitting at the grand dinner table, next to each other just like this, how will you sit?"

"Like a man eating his dinner, Francesca," he said, gesturing at himself. Leaned back in his chair, one hand cradling a glass of wine, the other draped leisurely across his leg.

But there was something in his posture, ever so slightly leaning *away* from her. Rather than in. The thing about her station in life, being in her father's iron control, was that she'd spent a lot of time observing people. Deciding whom to mimic, whom not to be like. Watching conversations to suss out what people were really thinking or feeling so she could behave accordingly.

She might not know anyone personally who was desperately in love, but she had watched strangers lean into it and desperately try to lean out of it. And Aristide himself certainly knew how to portray a man in lust if not love. They would have to use that.

"If I was your real date, a sparkling jewel with a generous bosom spilling out of her dress like its own buffet, where would your hands be? Your eyes?"

His mouth curved in the way that had her stomach doing strange little somersaults, a feeling she had been chasing more and more with every passing day.

"Ah, you know my type so well. You must have been paying attention."

She ignored him, and the fact that her bosom certainly wouldn't be classified a *buffet*. "Your gaze would drift over her, and even if you had the control to keep that gaze from taking in the sights, you would look at *her*. You would touch her. Lightly. On the arm, the shoulder. You would lean in to whisper something in her ear. Correct?"

"Yes. That is what I *would* have done, as a single man trying to talk a woman into my bed. Not as a man who already has a bedfellow as we're trying to portray."

She shook her head. "It's the same thought process, you only alter it a little. You would still lean in, but perhaps instead of the neckline of whatever I was wearing, you would gaze into my eyes. You would lean into whisper something funny, and I would laugh, of course, gazing lovingly back. You would—as though you weren't fully thinking the motion through—reach out and touch the ring you gave me as if to reassure yourself our union is real, and not just dreams come true."

"My, you have given this some thought."

"No, I know how to set a scene, through and through. I know how to get people to believe the image. I have spent a *lifetime* learning optics. Now, let us see if you can accomplish this." She settled into her chair in her picture-perfect posture that she hadn't had to trot out in almost a week. She pretended she was wearing a heavy gown and jewels instead of a fresh face and a light sundress.

He studied her, eyes narrowed subtly. "You do that well, *angioletta*."

"What?"

"Put on the mantle of someone else."

"That's how I survived as long as I did. You will need to do the same if you wish to change years of debauchery into a beacon of goodness. Now, go on. Show me what you can do."

It took another few seconds before he lost that studying look. He didn't move, but he gave the impression of a more...*intent* than languid posture. Then he sat up a little, putting down his wineglass, and as his hand returned to his lap it brushed against hers on the way.

Electricity seemed to fission out from the contact—brief, almost nonexistent, and still her skin felt prickled with some kind of...heat. Instead of leaning back in his seat, his whole body angled toward her and he moved elegantly and seamlessly so that his mouth was at her ear.

"If you were not my wife, I think the whispers should be quite scandalous."

That was all he said, and still, her breath caught a little in her throat. Just the touch of his breath against her ear *felt* scandalous. Who needed words? Certainly not Aristide Bonaparte.

"But as you *are* my sainted wife, an angel among mere mortals, I suppose I will not mention that I would happily partake in any *buffet* you might offer."

Words and thoughts tangled in her mind for a moment. But this was...a party trick. He saw her as that stupid angel moniker. He wanted her reputation, not her. And those little innuendos meant nothing except to...

shock her, she supposed. Set her back a little, because he *did* seem to want distance.

No matter what his eyes said.

She turned to meet his gaze, hooded and mysterious. As much as she thought she understood why he did things, said things, behaved a certain way, she knew there was an entire mystery under all of that of who he really was.

And she knew it would never be her purview to know it.

"The goal is not to shock me," she managed to say, sounding prim and disapproving. "The goal is to make me laugh. *Demurely*."

"Ah. I may need you to furnish some *comedic* talking points that aren't shocking, then."

"I will do just that," she returned. She should leave it at that. Every rational part of her brain told her to leave it at that.

But there was some other part of her that had bloomed here. The one free to dive into the things she was interested in, curious about. There was no one here to tell her to be perfect, above reproach.

"Now you will show me how you can dance."

He leaned back in his chair on a sigh. "*Cara*, please. You must know I can dance."

"But can you dance with me? Can you make it look as though I am the great love of your life who has changed all your heedless ways?" She raised an eyebrow at him, all challenge. "I will remind you this is *your* plan. I'd be quite happy to never leave this castle and let everyone think you've locked me in a tower for good."

His expression went grim, irritated, but eventually he must have realized she was right, because he carefully stood and held out his hand. She took it and allowed him to help her to her feet, then a few steps away from the table to a corner of the dining room that could act as a makeshift ballroom.

When he stopped, he took her other hand as well, then adopted a position that might start a dance.

If they were brother and sister. He held her—at arm's distance—with enough space between them that an entire other person could fit right there.

"Aristide. You cannot be serious."

"Am I supposed to ravish you in front of an audience?" he demanded, clearly annoyed.

She shook her head. "You would not have your hands anywhere…untoward, but you would hold me close. Not as though there were some holy spirit between us for chastity's sake."

This got a laugh out of him, which made her smile in return.

Until he pulled her close.

It made breathing easily hard. It made everything inside of her seem to tangle into disparate parts and she did not know immediately how to proceed. He still held one hand of hers in his, but his other arm had come around her so she felt it, warm and large, on the small of her back.

He was so much bigger than her—tall and broad—like a glacier looming over her tiny boat. She thought this should feel oppressive, but it made her want to lean in. To find some shelter.

What a strange thought.

"Is this better?" Aristide asked, his voice so low it seemed to reverberate against every inch of her exposed skin. It shivered through her, and she was glad she'd decided to practice this, because she would learn how to…brace herself for this. This…physical reaction to her handsome husband.

And she would *not* let him see. She would not let her voice be hoarse. She would not let all these strange sensations show on her face. She had a feeling that would be…dangerous. So she met his gaze and spoke very clearly. "Yes. Much."

She tried to step forward, to begin the dance even though they had no music. It was a pantomime, after all. But he did not move with her. When she looked up at him with confusion, his mouth was curved in that ironic smile that made her wonder things about his mouth that she had no business imagining. Married or not.

"You follow *my* lead, *angioletta*."

"In dancing, yes, but in love, you must follow mine."

"All I know of love, so called, is that it blinds a person to everything sensible," he said darkly, moving her in a rhythmic circle. "Every other person, every need of their own. It is a…parasite, really."

"That is quite dire."

"Have you witnessed love?"

"Not intimately, I suppose." She did not allow herself to consider intimacy as her body moved in time with his. "I cannot imagine my mother loved my monster of a father, but she died before I can remember, so I could hardly say for certain. I've never believed it in the cards for me, so I haven't given it much thought, but we must consider it if we are to mimic it."

"Mimic what is essentially a parasite?"

She pulled away enough to look up at him. "I think the first step would be to not call love a parasite."

"Perhaps."

"Why... Why a parasite?"

Aristide shrugged. "All I have ever seen is it eat away at a person. My mother, for instance, loves and had an affair with a married man—who was cruel to all parties, I might add. And yet, she works there still. As his *housekeeper*. I have offered, time and time again, her own house, her own *life*, but she toils after a man who still pays her as the *help*. She calls this love."

"Maybe she is simply wrong?"

"I thought you did not believe in fairy tales, Francesca."

"I don't, but it was always nice to think they might be reachable for other people. Perhaps Vale will get his princess and all will work out well there."

"That would not bother you?" He quirked an eyebrow.

"I'd like to see *someone* in this situation happy."

"You may pursue whatever kind of happy you like, Francesca. Love is certainly not the only happiness out there."

"You are right." And he *was*. And he held her close enough that to all and sundry it would look as though they cared for one another. Just a whisper of a distance that spoke to the idea they'd rather close it, but that was between the two of them—not anyone who watched.

It was perfect, and she had the strangest coiling sensation inside of her. An odd kind of grief. Like they would fake this for years and years to come and it would never be real. Nothing would ever truly be real for her. Because whatever she was deep inside, whatever she felt was wrong and needed twisting into a better version.

She closed her eyes against such old, foolish thoughts she had hoped she'd banished when she'd decided to find a way out. Because other people got to like what they liked, feel what they felt, be who they were. She was not special in any particularly bad or good way. She was only herself, just like everyone else.

But it was strange and alarming to realize her great plans for escape and find that being on her own would still be so *lonely*.

Aristide stopped abruptly. "There. A dinner demonstration. A dance." He released her completely, stepped away. And didn't quite look down at her when he spoke. "People will no doubt be fooled by our performance. Are you happy?"

But she wasn't. She should feel some satisfaction. She'd taught him something, or he'd at least pretended that she had.

But she wanted to lean into him, to cry on his shoulder, and that was clearly *not* okay.

CHAPTER FIVE

RESTRAINT HAD NEVER been a word in Aristide's vocabulary. He liked excess. Going after what he wanted when he wanted. There were lines he didn't cross, of course, but he was almost never in a position to test those lines, because he didn't put himself in those positions.

Francesca was testing *everything*. He'd never once felt twisted up over *pretending* to be anything he pretended to be. He loved a mask, playing a role, but pretending to be her besotted husband twisted something sharp and ugly inside of him.

Especially when she looked as if she might *cry*, and he'd felt her tremble in his arms. Not because she was overcome with lust—he knew what that looked like, felt like. There was something deeper going on inside that woman.

He wanted nothing to do with it.

There were *lines*, and she wasn't meant to be of any interest to him. She was meant to serve a purpose, and he did not mix purpose and pleasure. She would be what he wanted, so he could get what he wanted, and in return he would reward her with all he could. Freedom and all that.

Not *interest*.

So he'd put her neatly aside. Physically, anyway. The past week seemed to take residence in his mind like some kind of fever. The triumphant smile when she'd revealed the cake she made with no help, that moment when their gazes had met. Held. The strange mix of joy and grief that crossed her face when she threw herself into the surf over and over again most mornings.

It was like watching someone being born. Realizing some great potential. She seemed to be sprouting before him like some sort of beautiful bloom. Like the pretty oleander that dotted the island—picturesque and fragrant.

And poisonous.

Because it felt like there were barbs sticking their sharp and tiny points into his chest. Every interaction with her felt like he was walking a dangerous tightrope. When she was only ever meant to be a means to an end.

And he did not touch his means to an end. He was not his father. Would never be.

So, the following day, he reminded himself of her real place in his life. He made all the arrangements to fly to Rome for a few days, followed by a trip to Milan, then Nice and Paris. He told his assistant to accept any and all invitations that came their way, as once they appeared at one event likely more invitations would follow.

They'd had their honeymoon, and now it was time to work.

He did not know why he expected Francesca to balk at this, to argue with him. But he found himself somewhat…shocked when she agreed easily to everything.

Quickly packed her things so they could drive to the mainland before the tide swept in, then got on the airplane that would take them to Rome with nothing but pleasant smiles and a clear attempt to get to know all his staff by name.

She was in as much "business" mode as he, and he did not know why that left him feeling *edgy*.

They flew to Rome, her curled up in a seat reading one of her new novels, enthralled and completely unaware of *him*.

While he brooded. *At* her. He hated brooding. He wanted to act, but he didn't know *how*, because the only action he seemed to *want* at the moment was touching her.

A line he'd promised himself he wouldn't cross. He'd never taken anyone else's promises seriously, but if there was one thing he prided himself on, it was keeping his promises to *himself*. To behave in keeping with the personal tenets he'd developed for himself, *by* himself.

It did not matter if anyone else saw it, believed it, or agreed with it. If he followed his own inner compass, that was all that mattered to him. No matter what rules of respectability, society, man-made laws, et cetera, he bent.

It had always been easy enough.

How dare this woman *test* him.

When they landed, he watched as all that relaxed enjoyment slowly drained off Francesca's face. This was where she'd grown up, and she clearly had no fondness for it.

He understood that all too well. Her expression pertectly mirrored how he felt any time he forced himself to visit with his mother at the estate of his youth on the peninsula of the island.

It made him want to offer Francesca some kind of… comfort. Reassurance. These were impulses he'd long since refused to indulge himself in, as offering solace and reassurance to the people he loved most had only ever exploded in his face. He could not imagine what offering them to someone who was a business partner at *best* would do.

He said nothing the entire trip from airport to hotel. He checked them in and took her up to a beautiful *honeymoon* suite in a beautiful luxury hotel in the middle of Rome.

Where he very carefully made certain their luggage was placed in separate bedrooms. A silent and clear message to her. Of what, he wasn't certain. Even less certain when she said nothing about it, or how it might look to the staff around them. She'd simply walked to her bedroom door and turned a sweet smile at him.

"Good night, Aristide," she had said, pleasantly.

"Good night, *angioletta*," he had replied. Irritably.

And he had spent the evening, once again, not sleeping. Then he'd gotten up early the next day and gone into the city center to do business. He had left word with his staff that he would not return until it was time to pick Francesca up to attend the ball and to let Francesca do as she pleased for the day.

At the ball, he would *lean in* to whisper in her ear at dinner. He would dance with her as if she were the only thing he could ever imagine laying his eyes or hands on. Because she was not *wrong* about any of that.

And maybe once it was all over, and he saw the response from the crowd he was playacting for, whatever frustrating discomfort dogging him would fade.

But when he returned to the hotel, to find her dressed and ready to go, all his plans simply…evaporated.

She wore a deep purple gown, form-fitting and regal, with hints of sparkle about the bust. Her hair was swept up in one of those intricate twists, and her makeup seemed to make her eyes larger, her lips plumper. Diamonds dangled at her ears to match the ludicrous one on her finger that he'd put there. She *sparkled* like a gem, and he suddenly felt like some kind of maniacal wizard who wanted to hoard all that magic to himself.

This was not what he'd expected. *She* had yet to be anything he'd expected. He was not sure he'd *ever* seen a picture of her with her shoulders bared, and maybe he had spent the past week watching her in much less, watching her swim, watching *her*, and he had not expected island Francesca to translate into the Francesca who was meant to give him respectability.

She looked like… Well, not the angel she had been presented as for long. Not some sultry she-devil, either. Just a beautiful, alluring, desirable woman. And still it threw him off his axis. Because he'd expected boring respectability. The elegant angel to save his fall from grace.

And here she was, looking a temptation. One that slid along his body like the whisper of a lie, hardening what it shouldn't, softening what it shouldn't.

He cleared his throat. Travel on the plane must have given him a touch of congestion this evening. "This getup is not quite what I had in mind for a ball to reinvent my reputation, Francesca."

She blinked. Once. Something crossing her expression that he might have called startled, and a little hurt, if he was cataloging her expressions. But the flicker melted away into that cool pragmatism.

"No. But I got to thinking as I shopped. I could wear the overly virginal gowns my father insisted upon, or I could dress to please myself. I thought, given the circumstances, it made more sense to choose a gown that pleased me. That might match *you*."

The words, and callback to her father's control, were a bit of a careful, polite *slap*, and he hated that it landed. Especially when she met him with that demure blankness that had been her go-to in the beginning, and he hadn't seen much of it the past few days. Like she'd begun to trust him.

When he couldn't possibly let her do that, knowing what happened when he allowed himself to think anyone saw any *goodness* in him.

"We do not want to match *me*, I assure you. *Me* is the problem. The point here in public is respectability. Was I not clear?"

She didn't move. He wasn't even sure she breathed. She didn't flinch or slump or look away. There were no flickers of hurt in her eyes. She held his gaze, cool and detached. When she spoke, her voice matched it.

"Is my dress not respectable?"

It was. He tried to be rational enough to accept that

it was. It covered more than many he'd seen in glittering ballrooms and galas. But there was something about *her* in it, for all to see, that made it very difficult to hold on to the rational part of his brain.

When he didn't respond, she continued. "Do you wish to pick out a dress for me? Tell me how to wear my hair? What lipstick color is appropriate for a woman of my station. Would you like to ration out my meals?"

"No," he bit out, irritated that she would use her father's controlling behavior against him. Worse, make him *feel* low and slimy when he wouldn't have thought that possible.

Because he didn't mind being low and slimy when it suited, but *she* made it feel *wrong.* "I trust your judgment of course." Which was both an outright lie and said only to placate her so he could get away from this *feeling.*

"The thing is, I gave this considerable thought," she continued, still so damn dull if not for the sparkle of her dress. "No one is going to believe you were immediately turned into a saint by the likes of me. It has to be more…gradual. And I think we'll both have to bend toward the other a little to get our point across."

"They will think I defiled you. *Ruined* you, the sainted angel of Italy. A demon drags down another paragon." Which did not matter to him in the slightest. If he cared at all what people thought of him, he would have lived his life like Valentino. But there was a line he now had to walk. And it wasn't so much *caring* what people thought of him, it was crafting it himself.

And she was… She looked… This wasn't going how

he had planned it, and he did not know why she was making things so damn difficult.

She shook her head. "Some may say that at first, you are correct. But dressing as though I am locked into some kind of chastity belt isn't going to change that if you're on my arm. We must make it look as though we've changed each other. For the better. I think that is the kind of story that will carry more weight, that will be more successful for you in the long run. But regardless, one ball will not magically transform your reputation after stealing your brother's bride. The only way to soften that truth is with a story of love. As we had already agreed, if you recall."

He did not know why it infuriated him when she spoke like that. Of stories and optics and what other people needed to believe. Like she had chosen *him*. Like she was in charge of helping *him*. Like this was all *her* doing.

When he had stolen her. Simple as that. She was supposed to be doing what *he* wanted, following his plans. Not making *better* ones that made too much sense. Not making this feel like a partnership when he never allowed those to take root.

"Shall we go?" she asked, all feigned brightness. "Or did you want to make a fashionably late entrance slightly...mussed."

Mussed. Such a prissy word. And he had to remind himself, no matter how she behaved, how she tempted, she *was* sheltered. Perhaps her father had been a controlling bastard, but that only proved Aristide's point.

She was out of her depth, and she was making him feel like *he* was. So he decided to return the favor. He leaned close, until her eyelids fluttered and her inhale was sharp. He waited for her to back away, but she didn't.

Which shouldn't be arousing. Shouldn't make him momentarily forget his purpose. He shook it away, that iron backbone of hers. The flush that spread over her cheeks even as she met his gaze with cool, dark eyes.

He leaned in close, so his lips were *almost* on hers. "Would you *like* me to muss you, Francesca?"

She met his gaze, steady and searching, and he realized he'd miscalculated when she didn't blush, didn't look away. Simply angled her chin, almost closer to this near-kiss, then dropped her gaze to his mouth.

"I think I would not mind finding out what that would be like, actually." Then she brought her eyes back up at him. And *smiled.*

For a moment, his brain was utterly blank. Nothing but the rush of blood, the tightening of his body, an alarming, deep-seated need that threatened to drown him where he stood.

So he said nothing, and she said nothing. They simply stood, too close, their breath mingling in the small space between them. The feeling of it slithered through him. That poison again. Weakening what he'd decided on, weakening what he knew he must do.

Keep her in the neat little box of *business* partner. Sex could be stringless fun with the right party, but this was not the situation to introduce nakedness, body to body. Not when everything he planned rested on her ability to pretend to be his perfect bride and lend him the respectability he *would* prove to the world he had.

Whether he did or not.

They would help each other, but they would *not* blur lines. This was the only right thing he knew.

So he drew his best weapon—cruel words and disdain—and used it. "I do not waste my time with senseless virgins who will likely get far too attached and have to be explained to how things between a man and woman work."

She blinked again, that one *harmed* blink, as if by simply closing her eyes for a second she could make anything that hit a sore spot disappear by the force of her eyelashes.

"Perhaps *I* do not waste my time with playboys who think they're invincible and throw little tantrums when they feel as if their power or control has been tested," she said in an even voice, mimicking his disdainful tone far too easily it seemed.

"Tantrums?" He laughed, low and bitter, shocked clean through that she would turn his barb around on him. That it would *land*.

Perhaps he should have been better prepared. In *all* of this.

"Tantrums don't have to be loud, Aristide," she said, like a scolding nanny. "Sometimes withdrawing is a tantrum all its own." She ducked out from where he'd all but caged her at the wall. "I think it's best if we're on time. One of those ways that I have oh-so-helpfully worn off on you that people might notice and comment upon." She grabbed a little bag that matched her dress but sparkled more.

She straightened her shoulders, met his gaze. All business. All certainty.

All *mask*.

He wanted to peel it away from her. Here and now. Layer by layer. Until she looked like she had after he'd kissed her at their wedding. Shaken and confused and out of her depth.

Exactly like he felt.

But as much as he'd built a reputation for himself as carefree and wild, he was not careless when it came to people. It was why he continued to get invitations, why he succeeded in business. Why people *liked* him, in *spite* of his reputation. In *spite* of his wildness.

Perhaps his mother claimed it was some kind of coping mechanism—coping with what, he didn't have a clue. Perhaps Valentino had—during one of their rare in-person arguments—accused him of keeping everyone at a distance with his vapid personality, as if Vale had any room to talk.

But Aristide understood himself and the world and people around him, because how could he not? He had built himself into all this, and you didn't succeed while drowning in denial. He understood himself quite well.

He could be the laconic playboy all he wanted, but he did not *harm* anyone who was perceived to be "below" him because he would never allow himself to be the kind of monster his father was.

Francesca *was* beneath him—in experience, in understanding—so he would keep his hands to himself and pretend the night away as her besotted *fake* husband.

Temptation be damned.

CHAPTER SIX

THEY DID NOT speak on the way to the ball. Francesca thought it was best for a wide variety of reasons.

She felt too close to tears. Not because of what he'd said. She didn't mind a few mean comments said in the heat of the moment, especially if she could return the favor without a backhand to the face.

Strange how even an argument felt like freedom when there was no threat of physical violence tied to it.

What bothered her was not the argument, though. It was that she'd let her guard down. She'd been so thrilled to pick out her own dress, to look the way she wanted to look and *like* the outcome. She'd been excited enough, lulled by the past week enough to believe Aristide *easy*. That he would go along with her at all turns. That he would give her that indulgent smile and compliment her on her choices.

But he was a man, and she should have known better. Moods were perilous things and his had changed last night. She should have known it would continue to threaten like a storm until it broke.

She would just have to get to know him better. Then she would predict his moods better. Then she would say the right thing to ensure they didn't have any more little blowups.

And you'll be right back where you started.

Except Aristide had gotten angry—though she still didn't understand why—and he'd yet to so much as grab her. She was not in physical danger here. He had given her that much. So she could learn how to…sail his tricky waters without feeling like she used to.

That was how she'd gotten this far in life with *everything*. It wouldn't stop now. She didn't have to forget herself, hide herself, be someone else to figure out how to deal with him. She could find *balance*.

That was the promise of a life without violence.

What was clear from his little outburst was that there was something that held him back from acting on any of his little innuendos, even when she offered. She did not know what it would be, but she would seek to get around it.

Because even angry at him, even hurt by his precarious mood, she wanted to know what it would be like to be swept away in the heat that swamped her any time Aristide was close. She wanted *all* the freedoms she could get.

Once she understood him better, she would.

The car came to a stop and she waited until Aristide came to her side and offered a hand to help her out of the car. She could already hear the low murmur of voices of people who were clearly recognizing him and anticipating the fact he'd brought his stolen bride.

He smiled down at her and camera flashes went off from outside the car. But she did know enough about him now to recognize *some* of the looks in his eyes. This one was blank, with absolutely no warmth behind it.

She slid her hand into his, warm to her chilled, and allowed him to pull her out into the evening. His smile dimmed a little at her hand, and he wrapped his hand fully around hers as if to warm it.

She tried to think of a time that anyone had ever tried to warm any part of her, particularly if they were irritated with her. And she was quite certain it had never once happened.

She blew out a breath as he drew her into the fray. She had to focus not on him right now, but on the situation. She was an old pro at acting and presenting exactly what she wanted to project.

But no one had ever been holding her hand while she had to project anything. Even the events she'd attended with Vale hadn't included hand-holding. But she liked to think she'd learned something from being his fiancée while the press kept beating the Princess Carliz drum.

It didn't matter what the reality was. It mattered what the *story* was.

She and Aristide were a story.

She just wished she felt the same sort of distance from Aristide that she had felt with Vale. They were both handsome, powerful men. Who looked quite a lot alike, in fact, so Francesca didn't quite understand why it *felt* different. Only that it did. For her, anyway. She wasn't sure what Aristide felt. Some attraction…maybe. But there was a simmering anger or frustration that went along with it that she did not understand.

"Perhaps, like usual, you are simply not good enough."

She rolled her shoulders, willing her father's voice away. She would damn well be good enough. She would turn around Aristide's reputation quickly and easily. And he would *have* to be impressed by it. And her. Maybe then… He would act on what arced between them.

Aristide led her straight to Signora Gallo and greeted her with an enthusiasm she knew was forced, and the skeptical look on Signora Gallo's face told Francesca the older woman knew it too.

The signora looked over at her, gave her an up-and-down perusal. Then sniffed. "Well, marriage agrees with you, I suppose."

Which was a far cry from her usual greeting of feigned politeness: *Do you even eat, dear?*

The signora's gaze turned to Aristide. "Not quite sure how you pulled off such a thing, or why, when everyone knows you've never kept an eye from wandering."

Aristide kept that smile on his face. All charm and ease. *A lie*, she wanted to hiss at him just to see how he might react.

"That was all before I met *mio angioletta*. Why would my eye wander from a prize such as this?" He looked over at her, and Francesca wondered if anyone else noted that wry twist to his smile. "Who puts up with my wicked ways and encourages me to be better."

"And I assume you encourage her to be worse."

"Not worse," Francesca corrected gently. "Aristide allows me to be myself. It's…irresistible."

The older woman studied Francesca for a long-drawn-out moment. "That is a gift," she said carefully, almost reverently. But then her smile sharpened. "If it's true."

"That was the difference between my brother and me, naturally," Aristide's said, and Francesca wanted to groan. Because he should *not* bring up Vale if they wanted the stories to rehabilitate him. "*I* could see Francesca for who she truly is."

The signora made a *hmphing* sort of noise. "And I suppose you are why your brother refused my invitation tonight?"

Aristide laughed, and it was only a *tinge* bitter. "Signora, were you trying to cause trouble with your invitations? For shame."

She looked almost amused, but then she waved them away in her usual way of dismissal. Another group of people arriving for her to poke at.

"Did you really need to mention Vale?" Francesca whispered at him as they walked toward their table. "That little story will end up in print somewhere before the night is even through. We don't have to make *him* look bad to make us look good."

"Let him twist in the wind for once. He's done it plenty to me." Aristide plucked two flutes of champagne from a passing tray, handed her one.

"It seems to me you've done plenty to each other. Without ever once *talking* it through," Francesca added, lifting the glass to her mouth and taking a sip.

He gave her a sharp look. "You do not know anything about my brother and me."

A touchy subject. Her entire life she'd spent tiptoeing around touchy subjects, but something about Aristide made her want to *touch* everything. It didn't matter she knew she shouldn't put a fork in an electrical outlet—there was a desire to do so that was impossible to ignore.

"You'd be surprised what I know, having spent some time with both of you and watching how the two of you react to one another while your detestable father plucks the puppet strings."

"You are *my* wife, Francesca. I believe that means you no longer get to take Vale's side on anything."

"It does not mean that, but even if it did, I'm not taking his side. Or yours." She reached out and put her hand on his shoulder, wanting to comfort even as she wanted to poke. "I'm saying I think it'd behoove you both to talk. I know if I had a sibling to discuss my terrible—"

It was as if even *thinking* about mentioning her terrible childhood, the perpetrator of it appeared.

"Francesca," her father greeted, his dark, hard gaze landing on the drink in her hand disapprovingly. "It seems you have weathered the events of the week quite well." He did not say this kindly, even though he'd turned his gaze to Aristide and plastered that smile that fooled everyone on his face.

Francesca swallowed, her arm falling off Aristide's shoulder. She had to fight the slight tremor that went through her. The abject *fear*, even knowing she was safe here in a crowd of people.

But not just *here*. She was free now, all the time, and still she felt pinned to the spot. Like one wrong move would be a disaster. Her throat clogged and her entire being iced straight through.

She had thought once she was free of her father, dealing with him would not feel this way. So much *fear* still pounding through her, even though she *was* free.

But Aristide's hand over hers was one point of warmth in all this cold and she focused on that so she could find her voice.

"Allow me to introduce my husband, Aristide Bonaparte." She knew her smile wasn't right. It was too tight, too brittle. But she managed to curve her mouth as she gestured to Aristide next to her.

Bertini held out his hand for Aristide to shake. "I think we have quite a lot to talk about, young man."

"Do we?" Aristide countered. He looked at the outstretched hand and very clearly and purposefully did not shake it. "I don't think we have anything to discuss at all, Signor Campo. In fact, I think it best for all involved if I never see you again." Aristide said this all with an easy smile, so easy and friendly it took Francesca a good beat or two to realize what he'd just said.

She should say something. Admonish him. They were in public. They should all pretend. But she could only stare up at him in wonder.

"I beg your pardon," Bertini replied, clearly needing the same time Francesca had to understand what was happening.

Aristide leaned down, close to her father, but still with that pleasant smile on his face. "If I ever see you within eyeshot of my wife, you will regret it. If you need the threat specified and in writing, I'll be sure to deliver it first thing in the morning."

Bertini's eyes narrowed. "You signed the marriage contract. You have paid me my fee. You do not get to—"

"I think you'll find I *get to* do whatever I want, seeing as I paid your fee. And I won't feel the need to destroy you, as long as I never see you in her orbit or mine again. Understood?"

Francesca watched as her father's face mottled red. She felt the familiar ice of terror, and even Aristide's hand in hers could not feel like a warm spot. The only thing keeping her upright and from scrambling away was knowing she was not going home with her father tonight. He could not hurt her.

Because she suddenly had this...protector. She did not understand where it came from. Surely Aristide didn't know the full...extent of her father's control from the few things she'd said. She had always been careful to keep it from everyone.

She'd let Aristide in on how controlling he could be, but surely he didn't understand...

Aristide pulled her away from her father. If anyone had been paying attention—and no doubt, some had—there was no missing the fact that *something* had occurred. Though Aristide had kept that pleasant smile on his face for the whole strange interaction, so many of the gossips would have a difficulty deciding what the issue was.

Francesca realized her teeth were chattering. What a silly reaction to *nothing*. Aristide led her to a little corner, somewhat hidden and shaded by some ridiculously overlarge plant. She leaned against the wall, trying to get a hold of herself.

Aristide took the champagne flute away from her, then took both her hands in between his. He rubbed warmth into them. This same man who'd been angry with her not an hour ago.

It was all just *too* much. So she focused on the current issue.

"You probably shouldn't have refused to shake his hand," she managed weakly. Even though she was glad of it.

"I will not abide bullies, Francesca." He rubbed her hands between his, somewhat absently as he tracked Bertini's movements throughout the large ballroom from their little corner. All the way to the exit. Like her father was leaving.

Because of what Aristide had said. Done. She found herself managing easier breaths, but she couldn't stop staring at the man who'd just…stepped in and *done* something.

After a while, Aristide's gaze came to land on her. She wasn't sure what she'd expected—frustration, confusion, maybe even pity. But all she saw was a considering kind of searching in his gaze.

At first, she thought he'd say nothing and they could move on from this as though it had never happened. But after a few ticking minutes, as though he were waiting for her to get ahold of herself again, he spoke.

"My father could not care about anyone beyond himself enough to lift an actual physical finger to them. He much prefers mind games for his brand of cruelty, and that can cause fear, I suppose. But I have never felt the kind of fear I saw in your eyes when your father said your name."

She wanted to *cry*. Had anyone been even the slightest bit concerned that she was afraid of her own father in her entire life? She didn't think so. Granted, she'd learned early on to hide it lest the punishment be worse, but still. This was…too overwhelming.

"I will not abide it." He said this softly, but like a vow. More serious than even the ones they had given each other on their wedding night.

She managed to blink back the moisture in her eyes. "Thank you," she said thickly, but with feeling because… Never. Never had someone said anything like that to her. And this man might be her husband whom she was still trying to get to know. They might be friendly and have chemistry, but he was essentially… a stranger. Who wanted to keep her at arm's length. He certainly didn't owe her much.

He grunted, clearly uncomfortable with her raw gratitude. She wasn't exactly comfortable with it either, but she was still shaky enough she couldn't build back her defenses.

She really thought she would have been cured by freedom. It was lowering and frustrating to realize she wasn't. And something akin to joy to know someone would step in anyway.

"Would you like to leave?" he asked her gently. This man who said no one had ever called him *kind*. Who had been so irritated with her choice of dress, and the fact she'd had the gall to say she wouldn't mind being mussed by *him* that he'd called her a senseless virgin. Who was now…standing guard of her like some sort of shining knight.

He made no sense, but she wasn't sure she made any

sense either. She sucked in a deep breath and tried to settle all the things shifting around inside of her.

She managed to shake her head. "No, it's better to stay until we can make an early exit look less about my father and more about..."

"Not being able to keep our hands off each other?"

"Yes. Precisely." She gave a sharp nod and pushed herself off the wall. "We will dance and convince everyone we're madly in love."

Even if the word *love* tasted like ash in her mouth.

Aristide held Francesca gently in his arms as they moved to a slow, classical waltz. In direct contrast to last night, when she had felt like a strong, dangerous threat, tonight she felt...fragile.

He did not *do* fragile, because it made him feel like this. Unwieldy and wrong. *Not* in charge of his own fate, because the fate of the victim was more important.

And this all took him by such surprise, even knowing he hadn't liked her tales of her controlling father. He'd known he wouldn't *like* Bertini Campo, but then he'd seen her reaction to her father.

All her commentary, her even looks, all her *strength*, it had crumbled under the gaze of *one* man. Her own father. And he had seen *true* fear there in her eyes.

And for a second, he'd seen himself as a boy. Not with his father, because Milo Bonaparte had been a strange figure in his life. A complete nonentity for twelve years, and then a sudden target, but even as a young man reeling from his new place in the world, he had always known Milo's barbs—even the ones aimed at Aristide—were meant for Valentino.

And so his *crumble* had come at the hands of his own brother, his best friend, who'd called him a liar at the lowest point he could remember. Who had promised they would *never* really be brothers. All because it didn't fit in with his neat version of what the world was.

That moment might have changed his life, but there'd been an honesty in it. *Finally.* Valentino had chosen who he really wanted to be, and so Aristide had chosen the same. And maybe, *maybe*, Francesca wasn't far off. They hadn't talked since that moment. Not really. Perhaps there was more to it all, what with the fact they'd been *boys*, not men.

But Aristide was hardly going to throw himself at the brick wall of Valentino. He'd already spent too much time throwing himself at the brick wall of his mother.

Brick walls were hard and painful, and he saw no reason to indulge. He was not after his own destruction, or the destruction of anything else.

Still, he did *not* abide bullies, not because of his brother, of that moment Valentino had turned on him. It was the way his father used that moment of contention between brothers from then on out. Like a weapon against both of them. No, Aristide could not stomach those who wielded their power like a weapon—be it physically or with schemes—because that was the purview of his father. And he'd always counted his father one of the worst monsters he could imagine.

But a man who would inspire that kind of fear in his

own daughter was far worse than cruel, distant fathers and soul friends turned blood enemies.

All of Francesca's talk about being free now seemed... serious. Not the frivolous talk of a girl who'd had a slightly overbearing upbringing. But a woman who had escaped *abuse*. On her own terms, even if he'd stepped in and altered them a little.

She was *changed* to him now, and he did not know how to move forward. It was unfair, like being thrust back in time, to thirteen and lost and everyone he'd thought he could lean on crumbling under the weight of secrets come to light.

"You should probably not look as though you want to burn the place down while we dance," Francesca murmured in his ear.

She was back to herself. Stiff-spined and determined. It rearranged everything inside of him, in new, uncomfortable ways he didn't want. He felt *clumsy*, when he had known how to turn a woman about a ballroom almost as if he'd been born with the inherent talent.

He looked down at her and had to wonder if that crumbling he'd seen in her had simply been a mirage. Maybe he'd overreacted. "Did he lay a hand on you, Francesca?"

She inhaled sharply. "I'd rather not discuss him at the moment."

"I know nothing of what a good father should be, but I certainly know one shouldn't lay a hand to his daughter."

She was stiff in his arms now, and he thought back to all her discussions of the kind of *image* they should portray. So he drew her closer, to hide that stiffness. Certainly not to comfort her.

"Your father *never* laid a hand on you?" she returned, looking up at him with challenge and irritation in her eyes. She had not wanted him to press the issue, but he found he could not drop it. Not for a better time.

He held her gaze. Maybe someone would see it as *loving*. He was only going for the truth. "No. He had his own weapons, but his hands were not one of them."

She let out a shaky exhale, even as she kept that stubborn chin lifted. "I did not think seeing him would affect me, as I am no longer under his control. Unfortunately, that was not the case." She straightened those shoulders, gave him that boardroom-businesswoman look that had no bearing when discussing *abuse*. "But I will get better at it."

The fact she thought *she* should be better at it, when her father was the monster, twisted through him. He had seen the abuses of power and words and threats and control, not physical ones, and yet it all felt the same in the moment.

He had never once been able to convince his mother she was a victim, that she needed to escape. The fact Francesca had designed her own escape, even if he'd upended her plans a bit, awed him.

"We will not be anywhere he is, ever again. I will ensure it." Perhaps he said it more forcefully than necessary. Perhaps his grip on her was tighter than it needed to be as they swayed in time with the other dancers.

But this was one thing he would ensure, no matter what. As a matter of...well, those lines he drew for himself. He was not *virtuous*, but he would not let people suffer at the hands of those more powerful.

She studied him then, a hint of vulnerability in the cast of her mouth. "I am not weak," she said softly but with a resolute determination that twisted painfully inside of him.

Painfully enough, he was surprised to hear his own words emerge as gently as they did. "No, *angioletta*, that is never the word I would use to describe you."

She was still studying him, brows drawn together. "I do not understand you, Aristide," she said, almost on a whisper. And no doubt the lookers on would see a woman whispering sweet nothings to her husband.

So he lowered his mouth to her ear, being careful not to inhale the scent of her too deeply. "Let us not concern ourselves with *understanding* one another. Instead, we shall offer each other that which we need. A new reputation for me. Freedom for you."

When he straightened, her gaze was steady. There was no more hint of vulnerability. There was that same look in her eye she'd had last night.

"I think you should kiss me," she said, pressing closer to him. Sending twin reactions through him. The need to hold her tighter, press her closer. The need to stiffen and set her aside.

But she kept talking as she rested her forehead against his cheek while they swayed their way into another song. "There is a camera right there. It's the perfect photo op."

CHAPTER SEVEN

FRANCESCA'S HEART BEAT loudly in her ears. She was on shaky ground. Touched at the way he'd handled her father, confused by the seemingly disparate reactions he had to her. No one ever in her life had acted the role of protector. She'd never asked anyone to.

Yet he'd stepped in like it was his sworn duty—when she would have...crumbled. Not forever, but briefly. Apparently, freedom didn't *cure* the scars left behind.

And that was part of the shaky ground—that she wasn't as *cured* as she might have liked to be. That someone had seen that in her. But then that someone had stepped in to...help.

As she had told Aristide, she was not weak. She hadn't allowed herself to be for some time. She had come to a determined conclusion as a teenager, sporting a painful bruise that had swollen her eye so badly she hadn't even been able to hide it with makeup, that the only way she escaped abuse altogether was to make that escape happen *herself.* No one was coming to save her.

And so she had saved herself. Carefully and methodically over *years*.

She figured this was the key to success in all things.

But Aristide seemed to want to…protect her in some way, and it felt like perhaps in this phase of her life weakness wasn't so bad. Because in her moment of weakness, there could be someone who stepped in and took care of it.

Just as she would take care of his. His reputation.

She *did* suggest the kiss because she'd seen the photographer, because she was determined to succeed *for* him, even more so after this evening, but even in this moment she knew she'd also suggested it because she wanted to feel his mouth on hers.

She did not understand him or her reaction to him, but she wanted to.

In a world of things beyond her control, figuring people out was the one thing she'd learned how to hone. How to use. She would figure out a way to use it on him, so everything worked out.

Everything.

He inclined his head down toward her. His dark eyes were inscrutable. Something…*something* glittered behind that careful mask, but she could not read it or reach it, even as he brought his mouth to hers.

She held his gaze, though her eyes wanted to flutter closed. Because watching him as he kissed her was a revelation. When she'd closed her eyes in the chapel, she'd gotten lost in the sensation, let it overtake her. There had been a humming wonder in that, but it had also sort of…happened *to* her.

Now she wasn't just aware of his mouth on hers, but of where they were. That there were eyes on them, that a camera was likely taking their picture. She could feel the points of heat that were his palms on her lower back, the soft swipe of his lip against hers—a friction that frazzled through her even as his dark, dark gaze kept her pinned to the spot. She could feel the strength of his muscles under her own palm, watch his eyes darken there before her, feel his heart beat against hers.

It lasted no more than a few moments. Brief and full of yearning—at least from her. When he pulled back— not just his mouth, but his entire body—she could not call what she'd felt in him a *tremor* exactly, but it had been some sort of reaction. Elemental, maybe.

They affected each other, and *this* was like a hit of some kind of drug. She wanted to keep finding the more expansive high.

He did not release her, but the remainder of the dance was kept at enough distance their bodies barely brushed. The entire time, she studied him, trying to understand how her body could simply…alight, when that kiss had been nothing special, and for a photo op only.

She did not believe in love, at least not for someone like her. But she knew passion existed. She'd seen it starkly in the difference between the way Vale had looked at her and at the Princess everyone was so sure he really loved.

Maybe he'd never acted on that passion in his gaze, maybe he had. She'd never considered it much of her business. But she knew it was *there*. And as she hadn't felt it for him, she'd never been particularly jealous of it. It was more an obstacle to overcome so their union worked in her favor.

Now it was somehow the swirling center of her and

Aristide—the man who was supposed to give in to any passion that came his way. But he kept her at this strange, irritable distance any time that passion seemed possible.

Once the song ended, he ushered her off the dance floor and spent the rest of the night whisking them from one conversation to the other. He laughed, he chatted. He introduced her to people, and she introduced him to some. On the outside, they appeared a perfectly happy newlywed couple, she knew.

But she also sensed something simmering beneath the surface. One of those *moods* she was going to have to get to the bottom of so she could navigate. So she could work things out.

The moment they were alone in the back of his car together, his mask fell. That lazy smile, that sparkle in his eyes, all gone. He made sure there was a distance between them in the car—not just physical, but as though his internal life was as far away from her as possible.

Francesca knew how to read a Do Not Disturb sign someone put out. She had always heeded those. Poking into people's dark spaces was risky. Francesca was not one to take a risk, because you needed a bedrock of safety from which to take risks from, and she'd never had that.

After tonight, Aristide felt like that safety. Because she'd seen him angry, and he hadn't hurt anyone. Because he seemed so viciously and vehemently against the idea of a father raising a hand to his daughter.

He could scoff at the idea of kindness, but he'd shown

her his ability for it, over and over again. So, she risked. She scooted closer to him. "Is something amiss?"

He looked over at her, not outright scowling but with something *accusatory* in that expression of his. "What would be amiss?"

"I don't know. That's why I'm asking."

"All in all, I think tonight was a grand success. A good kicking-off point." He smiled. Thinly. "And many more events to go yet to reach that end goal."

She supposed if he wanted to talk business, she could oblige. She had some thoughts on the events he'd planned thus far. "We will need to add some charitable outings, I think. To lend credence to your change. It should be something personal to you. So when people see the photo op, it feels *personal* and not like an image cleansing."

"I don't particularly like using charity to help my personal gain."

"Don't be ridiculous." She waved this strange bit of morality away. "Everyone does it, and it's not just personal gain. Whatever face time you give a charity helps that charity with publicity, which often translates into more donations. It's only…slimy if you treat money like a cure, I think."

"I have *been* the charity, Francesca. No recipient of it wants the spotlight on them. I will not be party to it."

He said that the same way he'd said he would not abide bullies. All cold, determined certainty.

She studied him. This was *not* the image he'd presented everyone for *years*. These strange pillars of *nobility* that had suddenly come out tonight. "It amazes me that someone who has clearly spent *years* crafting an image pretends he doesn't know how to do it. You are *nothing* like the reputation you've made for yourself."

"Ah, that is where you're wrong." He flashed that playboy's grin that was meant to make any woman blush. She was not *any* woman, but she certainly felt a heat creep up her cheeks, a warmth spiral out from deep inside of her.

She thought of the way his hands had felt on her when they'd danced, their bodies brushing, his mouth barely touching hers for the cameras. If all that felt as good as it did, what might *more* feel like?

She scooted closer once more and that grin of his fell. His expression clearly read *stay back*. She frowned herself, because...he made *no* sense.

But the car stopped before she could try to puzzle it out, the door opened and Aristide slid out of the car like it was an *escape*. Francesca had never thought she might *throw* herself at someone quite so unmistakably and be rejected—obviously she'd never do it if all the signs weren't there.

But Aristide continued to be some strange mixed signal she couldn't sort through. It was frustrating. She *always* figured people out. She always got to the bottom of them and dealt accordingly.

She hurried after him. "Aristide," she said. She didn't have to tell him why her voice was all admonishment. He straightened, turned, offered his arm.

Because they were still in public, naturally. She took it and smiled up at him in the warm but dim light of the hotel's courtyard. He did *not* smile back. He walked with her though, if stiffly, her arm tucked into his.

In the lobby she leaned against him a little, enjoying leaning on someone bigger and stronger than she was. Besides, people were watching. She *felt* their eyes, saw the way they huddled with each other and *whispered*.

Once they got to their rooms, the door closed behind them, Aristide extricated himself from her grip. "Good night, Francesca."

"Let's have a nightcap."

"No, thank you."

She wanted to stomp her foot in frustration, but she kept her voice mild and her smile in place. "While tonight was mostly a success, I do think we need to work a little on our body language when we're mingling. You seemed to always keep me at arm's length when we were talking to people after we danced."

She moved over to him, took his arm and looped it around her shoulders. She looked up at him with a smile, angled her body so it brushed his as provocatively as she knew how. "We should stand more like this, I should think. Though not quite so...*buddy*. Perhaps you should put your hand—"

He abruptly removed his arm from her shoulders before she could guide his hand *exactly* where she wanted it. "I do not think I need instruction on where to put my hands."

She looked up at him, studying that angry look in his face that made no sense. Then she shrugged as if it mattered not at all to her. "It's only practice."

"I think we've had enough practice," he said gruffly.

But she saw the way his eyes tracked over her. Anger and frustration, sure, but he wasn't unaffected by her. He wasn't *uninterested* in her. He was just holding himself back.

The only reason that made sense to her was if the fact she was inexperienced made him uncomfortable for some reason, but that was foolish. So she did not back off. "Then let us do more than *practice*."

He stepped away from her completely, scowling. "That's enough, Francesca." The kind of fatherly scold she'd usually expect to be paired with a slap.

But Aristide was not her father, so there was that. But the fact he could remind her of those nights made her angry enough to forget her usual carefulness. She never came out and said anything that might offend, never asked anything of people that she didn't think they'd go along with. She figured it out herself. *Always*.

But he was making that incredibly difficult, so she wanted to yell at him, and her only defense against that feeling was to demand the truth.

"I do not understand this. You act as though you're attracted to me, but you seem to be…angry about it. Everything I know about you tells me you're not someone who gets *angry* about partaking in some chemistry. So explain to me why… Why I am *so*…repugnant?" She never would have imagined demanding an answer to such a ridiculous question. She didn't know why Aristide brought it out in her, but she could hardly take it back now.

Especially when he just *stood* there, so still and detached she couldn't help but think of his brother. They presented themselves as opposites, but she saw threads of men who were the same, even if she didn't understand how or why. Probably that father of theirs. If Milo poked at Aristide the same way she'd watched him poke at Vale, then no doubt they'd both built *some* of the same defenses.

"I apologize if you were somehow misguided about what this was, Francesca," he said firmly. Stiffly. "I will not, under any circumstances, mix business with pleasure."

And she understood it then. The line he had to draw. Not about *her*.

A line between himself and his father. Her heart ached for what he must have seen, knowing his mother worked for a man like that. Loved a man like that. Who would treat them both so poorly.

Maybe not with his fists, but Francesca knew full well that abuse took many shapes and sizes. She crossed to Aristide, even as he stared at her approach icily. Because she could understand this new strange pillar of nobility inside of him, but it was out of place here.

"I don't see this as business, Aristide. No money is being exchanged between us. You have no more power over me than I have over you." She held out her hands as if to demonstrate a balanced scale. "We are simply two people helping each other out. I do not know why it would be a *mix* of anything." She moved her hands to press against his chest, because surely he would have to see this line he drew just wasn't necessary.

She wondered how a man could look that cold and feel that warm. Carefully, he put his hands over hers—

but pulled them off him and released them so they fell at her sides.

"That is because you do not *know*. Playing the virginal temptress doesn't suit you, Francesca."

The barb landed as he'd meant, and maybe she should have left it at that. She would have, not all that long ago, but freedom had changed her. His protection had changed her perception of *safety*.

"You can throw my innocence in my face all you like, but it is only there because I have not had the opportunity to shed myself of it. I would *think* marriage would be the place one could do so, regardless of the feelings, or lack thereof, involved in the marriage."

His expression was cool, but his eyes were not. "Were you planning on *shedding* yourself for my brother when you were going to marry him?"

She supposed it was a fair enough question, though it really had nothing to do with anything at all. Because her marriage—to whomever the groom ended up being—was only about securing her freedom. Not about love or chemistry or futures.

But she had always assumed at some point she would share a bed with her husband—passion or not. She wanted children, and that was how they were made. So, yes, she supposed in some distant future she'd had the vague idea she might have to share a bed with Vale.

She had never spent any time fantasizing about it. It had been a to-do item on the checklist of her life, at most. Shoved to the bottom so she did not have to really think about it.

With Aristide, it all felt different, but she supposed *feelings* didn't matter. The truth was simple enough. "Do you want an honest answer to that question, Aristide?"

"I think you should examine why you would be willing to fling yourself at either brother as though we're interchangeable parts and what right you have to be miffed you might not get your way in the matter."

"You act as if intimating that I'm mercenary is an insult. I was not marrying your brother for *love*, any more than I married you for *chemistry*. We know what we are, Aristide. And I don't think I should have to say it, have to explain myself, but if you need to hear it, so be it. I did not feel attraction like this for your brother. I did not get lost in his mouth on mine, or dream about what it might be like to feel his hands on me. *That* is all you. All *us*."

His eyes had flared, and his breath seemed to be just a *tad* more labored. His gaze was hot, and for a moment she thought he might relent. Might step for her, put that angry mouth on hers. There was the faintest movement, like he was going to step toward her.

Then he gave his head a shake and turned on a heel. "Go to bed, Francesca," he said, low and serious. "There will be another party tomorrow."

And left her there, throbbing and frustrated, and more sad than she wanted to be.

But this was not something to be…sad over. He was wrong. She would simply have to prove to him that he was wrong, and then… Then they could figure out the rest.

＊ ＊ ＊

Aristide's body throbbed. It was *painful*, this want she stirred up inside of him.

He had never had cause to refuse an advance before, and the strangest part was he could not recall ever wanting so badly to take a woman up on one. He tended to prefer to do the advancing because he didn't like games. He liked to be forthright. He liked everything to be clear, so there was no confusion, no hurt.

Francesca was no *angel*, because she did not seem to understand subtle for the life of her, and it burned through him like some brand-new desire he'd never tasted.

That and the fact she had clearly stated something he shouldn't care about, but did nonetheless. That she did not feel the same desire for his brother that she did for him. When it didn't matter in the least what she felt for Vale one way or another. Because he wouldn't be acting on it.

But he liked what she said about wanting *his* hands on her all the same.

Still, this arrangement between them was too…complicated and confusing. And he knew that was the start of all hurt, all manipulation, all betrayal. The mixing of external goals and internal wants.

People thought him a libertine, but he had rules for *everything*. They just weren't rules like Valentino had for himself. They weren't about being *perfect*, about controlling everything within an inch of its life, or about how others saw him. Aristide knew how to bend. You did not have your entire life upended at thirteen and not know.

But there were lines he didn't cross so there were no victims left in his wake. There were chances he didn't take, knowing where anything with his heart, his expectations, his *hopes* led. This he took more seriously than *anything*.

He would protect Francesca. Give her whatever freedoms she wanted. He would even let her take charge of rehabilitating his image—because she seemed to enjoy the planning of it, and because she was good at it.

But he would not cross the line that would ever make her his victim. Or him the victim of what he felt for her.

No matter how much he wanted her.

CHAPTER EIGHT

Francesca woke up the next morning with plans upon plans. Some of them were very honorable. Arrange a few charitable excursions for her and Aristide in between the events he had planned throughout the glittering cities of Europe.

They could forgo the photo op since he was so against it, but they still needed to do the charitable activities and make sure the stories got around. See? She could compromise. On that anyway.

Some of her plans were of a more...*questionable* nature, she supposed. And did *not* involve compromise.

Because she was going to seduce her own husband when she knew very little about seduction. When he thought it was "mixing business with pleasure" and that was very bad.

Which was just so ludicrous. Their *business* was marriage, and making it look like they were in love so everyone thought Aristide a changed man.

It made absolutely no sense to keep their hands off each other when they both clearly wanted to know what it would be like, and it would only *aid* in their ruse.

When he had quite obviously had an alarming number of women in his bed before this moment. What was one more? Was he really going to have the only woman he *didn't* sleep with be his wife?

She understood his reticence, when his mother essentially worked for his father, even after having a son and all these years later. What a disturbing situation.

But she had *met* Milo Bonaparte, and Aristide was nothing like him.

Which made her realize, somewhat belatedly, that the woman who had served her and Vale tea with Milo when they announced their engagement had likely... been Aristide's mother.

She'd thought about that as they traveled from Rome to Milan, and there for a few days she played the role of a picture-perfect wife always looking adoringly at her husband. They appeared arm in arm, they danced, they charmed. And Francesca did not push. She let him put that distance between them, as if they were nothing more than *coworkers* while she watched him. *Learned* him.

She had not pressed him for any more kissing photo ops. She had dressed more on the side of that old modesty, as if that might lend Aristide some aura of sainthood.

It had not worked, and the stories about them had cooled. More interested in the fate of Vale and his princess—which no one could quite agree on.

"A picnic?" Aristide looked up at her from where he was reading a newspaper in a language she hadn't known he was fluent in. Because he liked to hide that part of himself. That he was smart. That he worked hard.

That at least she understood. His attempt to be the antithesis of his brother so it wasn't competition. She wondered if that was because he was afraid he'd lose, or if he did not *want* to be in competition with Vale.

While Vale's feelings on Aristide had always been centered in anger, Francesca had to surmise Aristide's stemmed from hurt. An interesting contrast.

But that was neither here nor there. She held the picnic basket she had put together herself. "We've done all the glittering parties. All the glamour. I think now is the time for someone to look at us in a…quieter moment. What better place than Lake Como?"

"We have a dinner to attend tonight."

"Yes. We do. Don't we want to prove to people we spend every waking moment together?"

He sighed, a bit heavily for someone this was all benefitting. *She* didn't care which reputation he wanted to trot out. As far as she was concerned, a good reputation never did anything for her. No more than a bad one would have.

But he got out of the chair and took her to the picnic place she'd chosen. She marched ahead, the scene already formed in her head.

She would lay out the picnic, they would talk, eat, flirt—hopefully. The photographer she'd tipped off via her assistant would come, snap a few candid photographs, and then leave.

She found her spot and spread out the pretty blanket and then set the basket in the middle. It was *beautiful*, and the pictures would be absolutely idyllic.

Then she looked back at the man who would complete the picture. He was dressed casually, as was she, and as she'd instructed. And still, the stiff posture, the suspicious expression made it seem like he was standing at the head of a meeting table rather than a cozy picnic with his new bride.

She smiled brightly at him and took him by the arm and tugged him into a sitting position on the blanket. She pulled the food out of the basket, handed him his share of things. There was nothing too fancy, both because she'd done it herself and by design. She wanted it to look rustic and homey to the outside world, as much as to Aristide she wanted it to look like…she'd put some heart into it.

Because Aristide might be determined there were lines and separations and realities and fictions, but Francesca wanted to try out what it would feel like for everything to be a reality.

She settled herself next to him, so their shoulders were pressed together and they could both lean back against the tree shading them, though sunlight dappled through like little stars.

The only way she knew how to make things happen for the better was to plan them out. To march forward, step by step, until the goal was reached.

And somehow her goal had become her husband.

She looked up at him. He was not *scowling* exactly, but he was looking straight ahead. It wouldn't do for a picture. *Or* for what she wanted.

There was one thing she knew got through that little wall he put up. She wasn't *proud* of using her trauma to get through it, to get to him, but right now she was determined to use any and all tools at her disposal.

Aristide knew he was too stiff. Her proximity did that to him more and more. Because she became more and more casual with it. A touch, a brush, her body next to his.

She acted *all* the time as if this were somehow *real*. She made this all feel *real*, when they weren't doing anything different than that honeymoon week. She baked him things, told him about the books she was reading, insisted he be there while she swam.

But something had shifted. From a simple kind of enjoyment to…understanding.

He knew her father had harmed her. She knew that Valentino had been the one to turn his back on Aristide. He thought he could see under almost all her masks now, though she trotted them out less and less.

He was terrified she could see under his—as he trotted them out more and more.

But worst of all, she seemed to enjoy his company, as no one he could recall ever had. Not just his charm, or his money, or his physical appeal. Not just…as part of their deal, but actually *seek it out*. She seemed to *enjoy* just being together.

Like they were friends.

Like they were more.

Sitting there in a pretty little sundress that she'd somehow made up to look casual. He supposed it was modest, but any millimeter of olive skin exposed made him want to see more. Made him desperate to touch, to taste, when he could never remember an ensemble any woman had ever worn to entice him having the same effect.

"I've never had company on a picnic before," she announced, out of the blue and with a kind of cheerfulness the words didn't match.

She was forever announcing these sad little tidbits of her life that made it feel like she'd turned his heart into a pincushion.

"You had *solitary* picnics?" he returned, hoping he was misunderstanding.

"There was a little place on my father's estate where no one could find me. I didn't go there often because I'd usually be punished upon return. But if I knew my father would be gone for a while, I would smuggle out little snacks and go there and pretend I was having a picnic in some beautiful park somewhere." She gestured at the beauty around them. As though she'd made her dream come true.

"Francesca. How *did* you turn out?" Because he had figured his way out of the slings and arrows of manipulation and meanness and rejection, but her childhood made what he'd always viewed as great trauma seem like a *joke*.

She looked down at her sandwich—one she'd no doubt made, as it wasn't neat or tidy like anyone he paid to feed them would have accomplished. "I decided to," she said, her voice small but firm.

"You are impressive, *mio angioletta*." She never balked at that name anymore. She *beamed* when he called her that. As she did now. Which meant he should stop, and yet...

He kept meaning to separate himself more and more from her, but watching her bloom in this new life of theirs was irresistible. Her palpable joy. Her confidence and determination. And what was the harm in watching if he knew what the lines were?

But every day she brought him closer to dangerous ground. Something bigger and bigger swelling inside of him. And he *knew* it could not take root or it would be a disaster for both of them.

He knew what it was to think so highly of someone. To feel those flickers of enjoyment and affinity and *need*. He had been very careful not to let these things into his life again, but she was changing everything.

He knew where that led. There was nothing he had to offer anyone that didn't cause harm. He had learned this at a young age and it had been reinforced later, so he'd grown into an adult, who made sure not to form attachments. It had been *years* since he'd felt this way.

And he couldn't escape it, because he'd married her. Because he could hardly turn her loose to fend for herself, and he still wanted the reputation she was crafting for him.

She looked up from her sandwich, offered him a smile, but her gaze dropped to his mouth.

Need slammed through him. No. Not need. *Want.* Because you could resist a want. You did not hurt people over a want. A want was a *choice*. And he did not have to choose her.

He told himself this. Over and over. Even as she seemed to make it harder to breathe. Harder to exist anywhere without putting his hands on her. His mouth on her.

"The photographer is here," she whispered, her eyes now searching his. Like looking for an answer.

He knew better than to think he was anyone's answer.

"Excellent," he replied, but he didn't move. Didn't look for where the photographer might be discreetly stationed. He couldn't give a damn about a photographer when she was this close, her eyes that dark, and everything about her simply *beautiful*.

To kiss her would be to give in. Cross a line. When he didn't cross those lines. He *didn't*.

But she tilted her mouth toward his, and she must be magnetic. The pull of her was too much. Something had happened in their time together, and she had *upended* something inside of him so none of the gravity that used to hold him center existed.

There was only her, and then the taste of her. Her mouth on his, gentle and sweet. Her arms sliding around his neck, melting into him. As though she was his. Some great karmic gift when he'd done nothing to deserve it. Her.

She was soft, safe and so damn strong it should humble anyone who came into her orbit. She set some hideous, needy, uncontrollable wildfire inside of him, and then soothed it with the brush of her hand over his hair.

It shuddered through him, and only the knowledge someone watched, someone took *photographs* had him easing back.

She fluttered her eyes open and looked so pleased with herself, and he wanted to be pleased too, but it soured in his gut as her arms slid off his shoulders and went back to her food.

He couldn't force himself to do the same. Lines kept getting crossed. Emotions kept swirling out of control. Something too close to *need* was taking hold when he knew it to be the enemy right along with expectation. Hope. Love.

But he didn't know what to do about it.

CHAPTER NINE

ARISTIDE WAS VERY cold on the way home, so Francesca gave him space once more. A few days of careful, modest, hands-off *wifing*. She didn't let herself think her plan was backfiring. If anything, it was working.

Just slower and with more fits and starts than she liked. But each time she reached out she got a little closer to the core of him.

He'd called her *impressive* and kissed her. She could live off that for a very long time. Here in this freedom she had now. She could reach out for and plan for whatever she wished.

Finally.

When they arrived in Nice, they didn't head to a hotel, but to one of Aristide's properties. He had another in London where they were headed in a few more weeks, but Francesca thought France was the perfect place to wage her own war, so to speak.

She gave him a day to settle in. To slowly warm back up to her again—because he always did. She supposed that was what kept her going. He was not *uninterested*. He did not actually dislike her or find her repugnant.

He simply had the wrong thoughts about what it

would mean if they found a way to make this real. She would show him the truth, though. Because it would be...a disservice to herself not to seek all that she wished now that she had the freedom she worked so hard for.

She wasn't afraid of hard work. In fact, she felt more settled with a goal, a plan.

So she would finally, *finally* seduce her husband.

The next afternoon, she invited him to sit out at the pool with her. For all the ways he kept her at arm's length, she knew he liked to watch her swim. She liked to imagine him weaving great fantasies about them, that he then applauded himself for not acting on.

It sounded like something he would do. Because she was slowly understanding her husband. Not everything he kept locked, deep and secret, but the way he moved through the world. The way he kept his true self locked under a careful mask.

She, on the other hand, had begun to get acquainted with her true self. She'd made them dinner last night— and had only slightly overcooked the salmon. She still did her swims, and she was reading through her books with great gusto. And in between all that, she planned their events, their image. Aristide's rehabilitation.

It was amazing to feel this free, this much *herself*. She wanted to offer the same to him.

So she would make it harder on him to hide away. To resist her. Because he wanted her.

She was sure of it.

And they both deserved the freedom to act on that.

So she did *not* dress in her swimsuit. Not even the *very* brief bikini she'd bought on a whim back in Milan.

No. She simply put the swim cover over her completely naked body and walked out of her suite of rooms.

Her heart hammered. If *this* did not get through to him...

Well. It had to. And when it did, she would finally know what lay on the other side of all this...unrest. And then...

For a moment she was rendered motionless by the idea that once she repaired his reputation, once she convinced him to act on this attraction between them, there would be no other end goal.

She'd have her freedom. She'd have made her payment, so to speak, to Aristide. She'd know what it felt like to have her desire met.

Then what?

She shook away that thought. It hardly mattered. There were always challenges to meet. No doubt new ones would crop up. Why borrow trouble?

She marched on through the beautiful house, all open and airy with lots of color and light. She liked his taste. It wasn't *all* ridiculous; he seemed to save most of that for the island and there was no secret why. Still, he did not choose a staid, uptight kind of dwelling, and it always brightened her mood. So many windows, and with the house tucked back into the hills, beautiful views always spread out in front of her.

She made her way to the backyard, where the pool stretched out toward the edge of their hill, so she could swim out and look out over the bay below.

She stepped out into the bright sunshiny afternoon, warm and summery still. She would have preferred a swim in the Baie des Anges, because she loved the waves and the surf, but the lack of privacy did not suit her goals. Nor did the name.

She was not anyone's angel, even if she got a little secret thrill every time he called her that, but she did not need to remind Aristide of yet another reason he seemed so determined to keep his hands off her.

Aristide was already here, stationed under a bright blue umbrella as he typed away on his laptop.

She rarely saw him work. He liked to tuck it away like a secret. She was fascinated by the way he did that because she recognized it so easily. Keep yourself hidden from anyone who might be inclined to look too close. Carefully keep yourself *safe*.

She was going to prove to him he would be safe with her. *Always.*

"You know, I'm not even sure I really know what you do," she said by way of greeting, meandering her way by his seat in the shade, making sure to keep herself and the very brief swim cover-up in the sunlight.

His eyes followed her, as they always did. "I hardly know myself."

Which was a flat-out lie. One of these days she'd get the truth out of him. There. Another goal after she achieved this one.

Buoyed by this, she came to stand at the chair next to him. She could have drawn it out more. She could have talked herself out of it, but she had gotten through life by making calculated, determined choices, and never second-guessing herself.

Because hesitation, second-guessing, uncertainty...

those so often ended in a blow. Literally. Better to be bold and true and certain.

So, without much fanfare, she lifted the cover-up off her body, just as she would have if she'd been wearing a swimsuit underneath. But she wasn't. Instead, she had briskly revealed herself to him. Entirely naked.

Her throat threatened to close then and there, but she carefully placed the cover-up over the back of the empty chair, trying to pretend this wasn't out of the ordinary. It was just doing one of those things she'd always wanted to do. Her heart hammered, and her nerves threatened to make her limbs shake, but she would not give in to it.

"I think you forgot something," Aristide growled.

She shrugged, very cognizant of the way the move made her breasts lift and fall. The way his gaze followed the move. "I told you I always wanted to skinny-dip."

"I believe you made certain to tell me you wished to do it *alone*." She knew he was trying for censure, but his eyes drank her in like a dying man desperate for water as she walked away from him and toward the stairs into the pool.

"I changed my mind. You can feel free to join me." She stepped onto the first stair. "The water is a bit cold, but it'll warm." And she didn't hurry. Didn't jump in. Even as her nerves hummed. She took each step slowly. One at a time. The cold water meeting the warmth of her skin like some kind of glorious torture.

And his gaze on her. Hot and heavy. She couldn't hold his gaze and manage this, so she turned slightly away from him, moving out toward the edge of the pool that would allow her a view down into the bay.

Water closed over her hips, her navel, her breasts. She hissed in a breath as her nipples tightened against the cold. Going from air to water its own cool, shocking caress.

What would it feel like if *he* touched her in all these places the water skimmed over her?

No. Not *if*. When. *When* he touched her. When he stoked these fires she did not quite understand inside of herself.

Because *he* understood, that much was clear. And he *wanted* to. Once he got over whatever warped impulses held him back.

With that determined, she ignored him for a while. She focused on herself. The way the water felt against *her* body. The way desire seemed to twine inside her, deeper and deeper, so that every stroke, every sink to the bottom and resurfacing felt like someone touching her.

But there was only one touch she wanted. She arched out of the water, letting her hair drip back before she blinked her eyes open to find him.

But he had not made a move to join her. He remained in his seat, fully clothed. Though his hand was now closed in a fist. He watched her, all tension and fury.

She only wished she could understand that fury. Why it should make him *mad* to want her, when she considered it a lovely little surprise. A boon, really. Who wouldn't want to *want* their spouse?

She blew out a bit of a frustrated breath. *Him* apparently. Because he still sat exactly where he was. Maybe he hadn't left yet, but he hadn't even made one little move.

She didn't pout, mostly because the impulse was foreign to her. Why feel sorry for herself when there were things to be done about the situation? Like, for instance, not hiding in the water.

She swam the length of the pool, back to the stairs, then walked right back out. She tried not to shiver as wet skin met air. Without looking at him, she went over to one of the lounge chairs and arranged herself, heart beating, body throbbing, starting to worry she would have to come up with yet another plan to make him break. She lay on her back, eyes closed against the bright sun above. The air settled over her, warming her slowly. She waited.

He would break. He *did* want her.

Finally, she heard a shuffle. She opened her eyes to look at him. He stood slowly, carefully, almost as if it hurt to move. Then he walked over to her, looked down at her.

So close, but not close enough. Not *touching*. Even as her breath sawed in and out, even as her skin *prickled* as the air and his gaze colluded to feel like very universes brushed against her.

He settled himself on the lounge next to her. Seated, not prone, but out of reach.

"I will not touch you, *angioletta*," he said darkly, and she wasn't sure whether him calling her *angel* was an insult or a praise. She found she didn't care because she liked it on his tongue either way.

"But you may touch yourself."

Francesca was the most haunting thing he'd ever seen in his entire life. All burnished gold and deter-

mined vulnerability. Dark hair and dark desires in her
dark eyes.

It took every last ounce of strength to keep his hands
on his knees. To not reach out and haul her to him.

Particularly when her entire body jolted at his words,
as if they landed in her like electricity. Her eyes wide,
her fingers flexed once almost reflexively as a pretty
little blush stained her cheeks.

And then spread lower.

A siren. A curse. She'd lead him to his death and
would it even matter? What could matter beyond this?
It wasn't a crossed line. Not yet. A blurred one, perhaps,
but he could blur it.

God, he had to blur it or he'd simply *die*.

"Go on, then," he said with a nod. "Give yourself the
pleasure you seek."

Her eyelids fluttered a little, and she shifted once,
with uncertainty. But she did not scoff, and she did not
get up, and she did not tell him to go to hell.

There in the bright afternoon sunshine, she lifted
her hand. Somehow he knew she'd be brave enough,
that she wouldn't back down. All spine and resolve,
his wife. Her fingers brushed over her breast, her own
tightened nipple.

He felt the touch echo within him even though he had
nothing to do with it. And still he stayed seated where
he was, even as he could imagine what it would feel like
to put his mouth where her fingers trailed.

Down soft skin, across goose bumps and into the glorious space between her thighs. Her touch was timid.
Halting now.

"Do not be afraid, Francesca. Be brave. If it were my mouth instead of your fingers, I would not hesitate to taste you. Long and deep."

Her breath shuddered out and he felt that shudder within himself. His body was hot, impenetrable iron. All tension and nothing but the hard, painful beat of wanting her.

She stroked herself, her eyes going hazy, her movements becoming erratic. And still she didn't close those eyes, look away from him, stop. She held him there, in her siren's gaze, a party to this even though he didn't touch her.

Wouldn't.

Couldn't.

She began to writhe, there against her own hand, the most erotic, beautiful thing he'd ever seen.

"Aristide." She said his name on a rasp, her gaze blurred with desire. The need to be the one who set her over that edge roared through him like a shrieking storm and still he held himself still and away.

"Let yourself go, *angioletta*. Now."

She made a keening sound, low and shattering. His whole body shook in response as her climax spread over her body. She was gasping for air, pink all over, and still she didn't look away. She didn't seem any less desperate. "Aristide, let me touch you. Touch *me*."

He would not. He *could* not.

But she pushed herself into a sitting position. "*Please*, Aristide."

And it turned out, she had the key to undo him after

all. Because her *please* upended him. Didn't just blur every line he'd set for himself, but erased them all.

And when she said it again, eyes big and liquid, reaching out for him, he let her find purchase.

CHAPTER TEN

FRANCESCA FELT MADE of sunshine. Heat and liquid and summer, swirling around inside a body that surely wasn't hers anymore.

She wanted it to be *his*.

There was a beat of a moment where she thought he'd set her aside yet again, but the *please* seemed to sweep through him like magic. When she reached out, he caught her, and then swiftly brought his mouth to hers.

And *plundered*. She was caught there against the cotton of his T-shirt, the hard, unforgiving landscape of his chest. All while his mouth took hers with no mercy, no give.

She didn't want any. She wanted the harsh demand of it all. The *certainty*. The way his hands moved over her as if they had a route in mind. As if he knew *everything* about her. The way his rough palm over her abdomen made her arch toward him. The way his mouth on her neck made her want to make sounds she was sure she'd never made before. Some strange kind of purring to encourage him to keep at it.

Every kiss, every nibble, every slide of his hand was some new universe opened up to her. Sparkling and vast.

But giving more only opened up the need for more. She pulled his shirt over his head, following whatever impulse took hold of her.

Like scraping her nails lightly up the large, muscular expanse of his back. When he growled against her throat, she laughed with abandoned joy.

Until he touched her, where she had touched herself. For him. The memory and the reality crashing through her, dragging her up that delicious, twisting tension in need of release. But just as she thought she might find it, as she strained toward him trying to find it, he took his hand away.

And it was his turn to laugh. Then he dragged that laugh down the center of her, his mouth a delicious tangle of new sensation until he settled himself between her legs and tasted her long and deep. Just as he'd said.

She hadn't known. She hadn't dreamed. All her life she had been tethered to earth, but Aristide cut those ties and let her fly. He didn't stop this time. His mouth explored her most intimate places until she crashed apart, with a throbbing, echoing *joy*.

As he moved back over her, she saw the flash of that detachment in his eyes. Like he might pull away. Like he might *stop*. She couldn't bear the thought. Not when they'd come so far. Not when it could be so much.

And she had found the key to this. If she felt him pull away, try to find that distance he was so good at employing, she only had to say one thing.

"Aristide, please." She didn't mind asking. Begging. Whatever it took. Because touching herself in front of him had certainly been a revelation in what passion could be found with only his eyes on her.

But she wanted his touch. She wanted him. She *needed* to know what more there could be. She reached for the pants he still wore, and he didn't stop her. He let her unbutton and unzip. To push them out of her way so she could feel more than the outline of his delicious hardness.

She touched him reverently, because it was a delicious thrill. To be this close to a man who could be so remote. To feel the most intimate parts of *him*, and know he was hard for *her*.

It was a gift to be so consumed with whatever pulsed through her that it didn't matter if she was naked or he was. All that mattered was that they found their way together.

"Please," she whispered again, meeting his gaze, one arm looped around his neck, one hand stroking the long, hard length of him. "Show me."

He muttered something dark that she didn't quite catch as he moved, pulling his pants off, so that he was as naked as she. All bronze skin and harsh lines. There was no laziness here in this body, no matter how he could affect the mask of it. He was all energy, all strength.

And for the moment, all hers.

He arranged her on the lounge, covered her body with his. His muscles tensed, his gaze fierce, and then him, there, slowly moving inside of her. Too much. It was all too much, and he was too much. She wanted to sob, but somehow in a good way. As if all releases could be good.

It didn't seem as though it were possible she could accommodate him, but slowly, inexorably, she opened, softened, accepted. Until he was so deep inside of her, she had no idea how she could ever exist again, empty and without him.

"So beautiful, so perfect," he murmured as she struggled to breathe, to process, to *still*. She had to move, she had to pant, she had to…

"So impatient," he said, with dark amusement in his tone. "When you have found such pleasure already. Luckily, greed suits me."

He moved inside of her like this was all they were and ever would be. Bound, fused. As if this was always where her life had been leading. Right to this point. Right to him. She'd escaped not to save herself, but to find him.

"Mio angioletta," he murmured there against her skin. Deep inside of her.

She hadn't wanted to be an angel, but she would be anything if he considered her *his*. To protect. To cherish. To make love to, just like this.

Stars seemed to explode around her. Bigger, somehow, when she would have said she'd already achieved every pinnacle of pleasure there could ever be. She shook, she sobbed, and when he pressed deep one last time, she gripped him hard and held him to her as he pulsed out his own release.

For a moment, they were still, shaking in each other's arms. She needed to catch her breath, her racing thoughts. Come back to herself. But before she could, he swept her up into his arms. And carried her, back into the house, through too many rooms to count into a giant bedroom that must be his. Because she got the sense of color and brightness, but she could not drag her gaze from his.

He placed her on his bed, looking fierce and haunted. She shook her head because she didn't want him haunted or hunted. She wanted him to feel what she felt.

Freedom. She got to her knees on the mattress, reached out and traced his face with her fingers. He stood stiffly, but not *unmoved*. No, he was trying *not* to be moved. Because his eyes didn't leave hers, and there were too many emotions in those dark depths.

But the one she recognized was fear. She had been afraid and brave all at the same too many times in her life not to recognize it.

She would find a way to reward him, for both. For this. For *them*.

It was like being worshipped. Pleasure, yes, so big it threatened to split Aristide's chest in two. But pain, because what a responsibility. To be that which this woman worshipped. Her fingertips followed every bone, every angle, ever line of his face. Slowly, gently, reverently.

And kept going. Down the cords of his neck. The ridge of muscle across his chest. Light, exploratory. Combing wildfires he did not know how to put out. Did not *want* to, if it meant she was the one setting them against every inch of his skin.

When her hand closed around where he was once again hard and wanting, he gripped her wrist. To stop her.

Surely.

But she shook her head, looking up at him with big, wide eyes luminous in the fading light of day.

"Let me. Let me show *you*," she whispered, and then said that word that made every vow he'd ever given himself and only himself crumble to nothing but dust.

If she begged him, he could not resist.

And then she followed every touch with her mouth. Soft and precious. Praise and veneration no one man could possibly deserve.

Until he was shaking. Until the need was too much to hold himself apart. He took her wrists again, this time to move her so that she was underneath him. He spread her soft, silky thighs wide and settled himself there.

"Say it again." He'd meant it as a command, but it sounded more like a raspy plea.

He found he didn't care when her mouth curved, a sultry smile tinged with sweetness that came from some secret part of her she'd not yet shown him.

And now it was here. Something she had found because she was strong and brave and wonderful, but something he'd helped her find. Helped her create.

"*Please*, Aristide," she said, somehow knowing exactly what he wanted, somehow sounding stronger and more powerful than any woman begging rightly should. But this was Francesca. His angel. Sent to save him or perhaps he would drag them both to hell.

It didn't matter in this moment. As long as he was inside her again. Where he fit. Where he belonged. Where he took his time, moving her close and closer still, but never over that edge she wanted again.

So she writhed there underneath him. Begging and perfect.

He placed his hand on her chest, fingers spread wide, the wave of possession so big and deep he wasn't sure how any man could bear it.

Then she moved against him, all her own. An arch up against him, and a roll back down And the sound of perfect pleasure that escaped her mouth was art.

"Go on, then," he said, watching her eyes, for that flare of everything that echoed inside of him. "Find it yourself."

She did not jerk at that as she had outside. She did not even pause. She arched against him again. And he leveraged over her, while she moved, set the pace, and raced toward her own staggering release.

She sobbed out his name as the sun set outside. As he lost himself and gripped her hips, thrusting inside of her once more. In a fever of body to body and gasping breaths and a climax so big and bright he thought perhaps the world had collapsed around them.

Since he could not hold himself up, he rolled to the side, and she fell with him. Somehow, fitting just as if she belonged tucked up next to him.

They both breathed heavily and said nothing as darkness engulfed the room. He listened as her breath went from ragged to even, as her clenched hand relaxed. Until she slept there, tucked in beside him, her head on his shoulders and her soft, thick hair seeming everywhere.

Aristide lay as the passion and energy of release

slowly drained out of him, as his own breathing slowed. As everything warm and good was replaced not with exhaustion, or contentment, or anything but a terrible, beating panic.

He had not been careful.

He had lost himself. Lines crossed. Complications created. All because she was a siren he hadn't been able to resist. And normally, he would not curse himself for a lack of resistance, but he knew she was...not understanding the situation.

Francesca thought this could be something. He saw it in her careful tending of him. The careful little battles she'd waged. Giving him space when he grew too cold, then pushing him again.

She thought maybe someday they could be domestic and happy. That chemistry could be love. That surrender could be strength. She had *planned* this, as she planned everything so carefully, so successfully.

But he had no doubt that instead of whatever dreams she was weaving, it would end with her crumbling in his clumsy, brutal hands. Everything that had to do with *love* always did. Trying to save his mother, telling Valentino the truth. Everything he'd tried to do in the wake of the terrible secret of his parentage had only ever ended in hurting.

She had now put herself in a place that allowed him to hurt her, and he could not forgive her for this. He had been *clear* what he wanted, what he needed, and she had instead gone after what she wanted with little concern to what he did.

And if they were to have a child because he had not *thought* beyond her *please*...

That had not been part of the deal. It had not been discussed, planned. It should not be *allowed*.

Something had to be done. Something more than a line drawn in the sand because he was weak and she was determined.

Sometimes, destroying the pretty thing before it bloomed was the only possible answer. And enemies had to be slaughtered before they could do the slaughtering.

Because he was nothing to be worshipped. He was nothing but a mere mortal.

What a pity.

CHAPTER ELEVEN

FRANCESCA WASN'T COGNIZANT of falling asleep, but she must have at some point as she woke sometime later to a rumpled, empty and unfamiliar bed. She pushed herself up a little, heart tripping over itself as she worried that Aristide had disappeared, but there he was.

Relief washed through her. He hadn't run away. He hadn't set her aside. His back was to her, looking out the window at a pearly dawn. But he was here. That had to be good.

Right?

She lay back in the bed, stretched out, enjoying the way her naked body felt on the soft sheets, used and slightly achy and his. Mmm. She was hungry. Surely they could eat something up here, and then, as it was a new day, see to pleasuring each other all over again.

And to think he'd been so against it in the beginning. So certain this would be a bad idea, and it had been *glorious* instead.

"See, that wasn't so terrible, now, was it?" she offered by way of good morning.

He turned then, but she saw none of that heat in his

gaze. There was only a bleakness that made everything inside of her go cold. Frozen, inside out.

"Did you get what you wanted, Francesca? Are you happy now?" He asked these questions not in accusation, but with a cold finality that shivered through her.

"I…" Instinctively, she pulled the sheet up higher as if to shield herself from that desolate look on his face and the ice of his words. "What?"

"I told you I did not cross lines. You understood why. So you crossed it for me. How good of you."

"Aristide." She was so shocked, so *appalled* at the way he characterized it she didn't have words beyond his name.

"If, God forbid, last night results in a pregnancy, we will deal with it rationally."

A pregnancy. He said it with such frigid disdain she couldn't catch her breath. It was like whiplash. Like an unexpected punch.

And she knew those too well. She hadn't expected one to come from him. Her initial response was to wince away, to hide under the covers, to *disappear.*

How *dare* he remind her of that old response. How *dare* he turn last night into something…cold. She pulled the sheet around her but got to her knees on the bed. "And what is *rationally* to you?"

"We will create another contract to discuss the details. Hopefully, it does not come to that."

Hopefully. Honestly, in this strange twist of events, she didn't know what *to* hope for, but… Maybe it wasn't the right time to introduce a child into the world, but she wasn't *opposed* to having children. "I do...want children someday."

"And it has become very clear to me that it only matters what *you* want."

Everything he said was so unfair. So off-base. And it hurt so deeply she was surprised she didn't just... crumble. But there was something about how well acquainted she was with the way everything was always twisted against her, she found anger swirled inside of her instead of defeat or retreat.

"What *you* want could matter if you would tell me. If you would be honest with me. If you wouldn't lash out with these accusations. If you had a *conversation* instead of always watching me from a distance. I have *tried* to figure out what you want."

"Ah, yes. I have watched you. Maneuvering me carefully. Exactly where you wanted me. Congratulations. You won."

He made it sound like such a loss she wanted to cry. Tears threatened and only a force of will built in the tragedy of her childhood kept those tears from falling over. "I thought we both won."

"Should you ever pull another stunt like that, we will immediately divorce. Reputations and contracts be damned. Mark my words."

"A stunt?" She laughed, because it was so breathlessly cruel, she couldn't seem to find anything else but a shocked kind of humor to it all. "I did not realize I forced your hand. I did not realize I had such *power*— me the *senseless* virgin."

"You begged me."

"And I suppose you've never said no before, so it must be my fault you couldn't muster it last night? *Multiple* times."

His expression was ice. Everything about it *hurt*. Because he made it sound like she'd *hurt* him, and she'd... She'd been so happy. So free. So sure last night could be the start of something *beautiful*. All her freedom a culmination of joy she—*they*—rightly deserved.

And he'd turned it into something ugly, mean and selfish. Tears threatened, but she blinked them away, still clutching the sheet to her chest.

Last night *had* been beautiful. This was... This was him being afraid of that. Afraid of this thing that bloomed between them. Because it wasn't just sex. It was *more*. Maybe that hurt him because he didn't want it to be more, but it wasn't fair to treat her this way.

"You turn your hurt into anger, like a weapon," she said. "And you hurt the wrong people. Because you're afraid what might happen if you don't."

"Ah, and what is this bogeyman I'm so afraid of?"

"That someone might care about you." *I care about you.* He had handed her a new world, just by listening, by watching. He had given her what she wanted. He had protected her.

And now he was ripping it away like she'd somehow...tricked him into it.

Because she had hoped that accusation might get through to him, might visibly land, but it didn't. He moved closer, eyes blazing with a fury that made her want to wince away.

"And do you know what I think *you're* afraid of? Letting anyone else have some semblance of control. You want to maneuver everything and everyone so *you* get everything *you* want and damn the consequences. Well, *cara*, I will not be your consequence. I will not be maneuvered by the likes of you."

It hit close enough to the bone that her anger wilted. Because she *had* maneuvered him. She *had* focused on what *she* wanted. She had ensured she got it.

And somehow that had ruined everything.

Aristide spent the morning working. It was not easy to concentrate, but he did it. There were things that needed to be done around his ridiculous social calendar.

They had a charity event this afternoon, followed by a dinner.

He wouldn't force Francesca to attend any of these events. Not immediately. They could skip a few things and blame those newlywed sparks. And if it turned out she was pregnant...they could miss a few more.

He did not let himself dwell on that possibility. Dwell on why it had not once occurred to him last night to do what he *always* did and protect himself.

Because once again, it had to be her fault. She'd started everything, begged him, been...utterly perfect.

He had not wanted to be haunted by the taste of her, the feel of her, the echoes of how she sounded when he tumbled her over that blissful edge. But they were there and he couldn't seem to eradicate them.

More than once he'd found himself on his feet, as if he was going to go hunt her down. But then he'd ask himself for *what*? To follow the contemptible footsteps of Milo Bonaparte to pick at everyone, bit by bit, until there was only bitterness or servitude?

It seemed to be the only kinds of relationships his blood knew how to have. And now he'd even spread that bitterness to his wife of convenience. Impressive, really.

Fifteen minutes before they would need to leave for the animal shelter Francesca appeared, dressed and made up appropriately. He'd expected defiance, that spark of combativeness he seemed to bring out in her.

She kept her eyes downcast, her answers short.

Everything about her was…different. This was not defiance. It was defeat.

But it was better now. Now, before anything could grow. Now, before she fancied herself in love with him or vice versa. They would weather this little speed bump and go back to the *business* relationship they were meant to have.

She said absolutely nothing on the drive over to the shelter. Her gaze stayed out the window, but the minute they arrived and he helped her out of the car, she was all warmth and smiling.

At the employees and volunteers, of course. Not at him. They were given a tour of the facility, and after Francesca so adeptly and politely declined to have their pictures taken even though she'd been the one to tell him everyone used charity, they were led into an outdoor area where dogs raced around, playing with each other, with volunteers, more dogs lazing about in the sun panting happily.

"We try to keep them as comfortable as possible while we wait to find the best homes for them," the manager said. "Your generous donation is going to be such a boon for us."

"We're so glad," Francesca said. And she was all cheer and kindness, but he saw a kind of *tightness* around her mouth. A little chink in the armor she'd put around herself.

It made him want to reach out and touch her, offer his strength, but he stood stiffly by her side, hands carefully to himself.

"One of the first things we bonded over was always wanting a pet and never having one growing up," Francesca was telling the manager. "But we're having trouble deciding on what would be better for our lifestyle. I'm thinking a cat would be easier with all the traveling we do, but Aristide just loves dogs."

She said all this with a cheerful smile, a slightly conspiratorial tone, as she leaned toward the woman who ran the shelter.

A flat-out lie told so effectively. Aristide wondered if he'd stepped into an alternate reality altogether, where this was all simply the truth. She was his and that was their past and they would have a *pet* together once they figured what would suit.

But not only had they never discussed his not having a pet, he clearly remembered her saying *she* wanted a dog.

"Something big and ridiculous. The more hair, the less brains, the better."

He stared at her, but she ignored him, talking with the woman about cat and dog breeds and the like. Aristide watched the animals around them, was distracted by one that was insistently barking—at an overturned bowl. None of the volunteers were paying the large dog any mind as if this was a common occurrence.

Aristide walked over to the creature, then waved to his wife.

"Come, Francesca. Take a look at this one."

With that fake smile plastered on her face, she walked over to him, smiled somewhat more genuinely at the dog.

"The exact kind of dog I always wanted," he told her with a meaningful glance, because for some reason he wanted to prove that he'd been listening when he should prove that they meant nothing to each other.

She looked at him as if he'd stabbed her clean through. Her smile faltered, but she knelt down to pet the dog. Who, momentarily distracted from the bowl, wagged its tail and used its giant, disgusting tongue to lick her face.

Francesca reached out and fixed the bowl, so it was now right side up. "There now. No more fussing," she said with kind admonishment as she rubbed her hands over its long fur.

But the dog reached forward with a paw, upended the bowl, and then started barking again.

Aristide frowned. "Definitely more hair than brains," he muttered.

And when he looked from the dog to Francesca, he noted she'd pressed her face into the dog's side. Her shoulders shook. Once.

She was crying into the dog's fur.

He had done that to her, and he had to accept that *she* was not the poison in this scenario.

He was.

CHAPTER TWELVE

FRANCESCA PLAYED THE perfect bride for the next few weeks. Sort of. She knew she was more bleak and bland than she should be, but she couldn't quite pull herself out of the little fog of depression. Still, she refused to allow him to cancel any events, though he offered most nights, somewhat stiffly.

No. They would do everything they'd committed to. She would do her *job*. If there was one thing she'd always done, it had been that.

Even with the cold, icy distance between them. Even with her heart shattered—of her own doing. Because he had been clear, and she'd crossed his lines for her own gain. She couldn't even hate him because she felt like too terrible a person to deserve the sweet anger that came with hate or blame.

They went to their dinners and balls and smiled and chatted and put on a good show. The stories in the press were even beginning to sway toward the story they portrayed. Just this morning she'd seen an article on one of those silly gossip sites titled "Could this Angel Really Have Tamed this Devil?"

But she did not feel like the angel she was supposed

to be. She felt like a husk. In her darkest moments, she pitied herself enough to think she'd traded one prison for another, but then she reminded herself no matter how much her heart hurt, she was safe here.

She could not *hate* Aristide if she was safe. If *she* had been the problem that had pushed them away from easy companionship and blistering chemistry to this horrible glacial experience.

She could only hate herself. Which somehow made it easy to put on the role of Francesca Bonaparte. Make up stories about who she and Aristide were, because there was no hope there'd ever really be a *them*. So she might as well make up a fake version for the nights they had to spend together.

Because in the light of day, he didn't eat meals with her anymore, and she didn't go near a swimming pool or ocean. She didn't bake or read.

They all felt like luxuries she didn't deserve.

Before they were to fly to London, Aristide approached her as she choked down her breakfast. It was no doubt delicious, but it tasted like nothing to her. She wouldn't have eaten at all, but there was still the possibility...

She tried not to think about how she might be pregnant. Tried not to look for signs. Tried to ignore it altogether.

And still there was a little flame of hope inside of her she couldn't quite extinguish. Just like the sight of him still made her heart flutter when she knew he would only ever approach with pain.

"We are taking a little break and returning home," he

informed her stiffly and from a distance. "My mother insists on an introduction, and it doesn't do to let something irritate her enough to complain to my father."

Francesca nodded. It was only a small change of events. They'd had a few things organized in London, but a trip home would be an easy enough reason to change plans.

She tried very hard not to think about how easy it was to consider the castle *home*.

"Very well."

There was the slightest hesitation, like he might say something else, but in the end he only turned away and left her there on the patio. Alone.

Exactly how you belong.

She knew this couldn't go on. All this self-pitying nonsense. She'd survived worse than being rejected. Maybe there was something to that. She'd never really had the time to sit around and feel sorry for herself before. Never got to just *marinate* in her feelings of hurt and inadequacy and mistakes.

So, now she'd done so. She needed to go back to finding her own personal strength in the midst of feeling bad about herself or her situation.

She returned to her room and packed, kindly begging off any of Aristide's staff who tried to take over the task. She needed things to do. Things that didn't involve Aristide. Or thinking about... She frowned a little at the twinge in her stomach. A twinge that usually accompanied...

She inhaled sharply, then steadied herself before going into the bathroom.

Well, problem solved. There was no baby.

She blinked a few times, surprised to find tears already falling. When it would have been a disaster to be pregnant. When it would have caused so many terrible complications.

"This is good," she whispered to herself. "An answer. Now you can stop being such a fool and get on with your life." She wiped at her face, but the tears kept falling. She did not know what to *do* with this reaction. She hadn't even lost anything. Just some fantasy possibility that had been nothing but a fairy tale.

And fairy tales were not for people like her. Survival was all she wanted. All she'd fight for. The rest was a joke.

She washed her face, finished her packing, and she met Aristide at the car that would drive them to the airport.

He studied her with that old intensity, and she pretended she didn't notice. Didn't feel it. *Business* partners didn't care how the other was feeling. Because there were *lines*.

She had never expected the lines to feel suffocating. That her freedom would feel like just another version of prison. A nicer one, all in all, but one that kept her from truly being herself once again.

Once on the plane, she pretended to lose herself in a book, though not one single word penetrated the fog she could not seem to fight. She didn't have to fake a nap on the ride from airport to island, because she was emotionally wrung out and exhausted.

When the car rolled to a stop, she awoke to find his

eyes on her. She pretended not to notice, though she allowed him to help her out of the car as he always did.

The sun was setting behind the castle, and the soft
sound of surf and the salty scent of it infiltrated that
little fog. It felt *good* to be back. Maybe that little week
they'd had here was just an illusion, but it had been an
enjoyable illusion.

Something about being back at his castle, that she
just…loved. Its ridiculous weathervanes and crazy
sculptures. The tremulous sea in the background. It
made her want to smile. It made her feel like she was
home.

But it wasn't hers and neither was he and there was
no baby to bind them, and she had to find some way to
be *glad* about that.

So she'd tell him. Flat out. She removed her hand
from his, met his gaze with hers, there on the walkway
up to the castle.

"You will be happy to know, I'm not pregnant." A
lump sat in her throat, threatening to choke her. It would
have been terrible timing for a child, and still she wanted
to grieve the fact that she was empty. Straight through.

He said nothing to this. Stood ramrod straight and
so far away and she had known he wouldn't comfort
her—he made it very clear he didn't want a child. But
she still wished for some kind of warmth.

And then she heard…a bark. Aristide looked over his
shoulder, and there bounded a dog out of the side door,
followed by a scurrying staff member with a leash dan-
gling from their hand.

"I bought you a present," he said gruffly, not reacting to what she'd said at all.

The dog from the charity event in Nice, at that. *More hair than brains*. She wanted to launch herself at the adorable giant ball of fur, but she understood far too well what this was.

Some sort of…buy-off. A distraction. Just another wall between them, but built using her soft feelings and wants.

She ignored the dog, looked her husband in the eye. "I hate you," she said, then turned on a heel and walked into the castle. Where she would lock herself in her room.

And if that was childish and unacceptable and all other things she'd never allowed herself to be before, well, then it was about time.

Aristide was glad to feel anger and frustration, because it was a nice change of pace from guilt and pain.

He had done something kind and she *hated* him? What sense did that make? He certainly didn't want a dog who escaped leashes and barked incessantly at upended bowls. He'd seen it as a peace offering.

I hate you.

He could not wrap his mind around it in any way, shape or form. Particularly as he stared down at the hairy beast Luca was attempting to get a leash on.

Surely she was relieved about there being no pregnancy despite their carelessness. She should be thrilled. He was. Surely he'd feel thrilled if he wasn't so confused by *her* behavior.

And *surely* her behavior didn't make any damn sense.

"Uh, what should I do with it, sir?"

Aristide grimaced at the dog but held out his hand for the leash. "I'll handle him. Thank you." Luca scurried away as if he was terrified he'd be stuck with the animal if he didn't beat a hasty retreat.

"You are *supposed* to be for Francesca," he muttered at the dog, then felt foolish for talking to a *dog*. "Come," he ordered, and began to walk toward the castle.

But the dog plopped its butt down and refused to move. Aristide frowned, tugging at the leash, but the dog didn't budge.

"Come," he repeated, through clenched teeth. He pulled on the leash once more and the dog did *nothing* but sit there and pant at him.

"Fine, then you can run away and see how you like fending for yourself." He nearly dropped the leash, but... Francesca might hate him now, but she'd certainly hate him even more if that fool dog ran off and got itself killed.

And what does it matter if the woman who crossed all your lines and only cares what she wants hates you?

He tried to hold on to that personal narrative, but she'd gotten too many of her own hits in that night.

"What you want could matter if you would tell me. If you would be honest with me. If you wouldn't lash out with these accusations. If you had a conversation instead of always watching me from a distance. I have tried to figure out what you want."

And she had said that so earnestly, with such naked

shock and hurt on her face that even all these days later, he hadn't mustered up a way to fight it.

He didn't want her to know what he wanted. He didn't want to have *conversations*. He wanted a wife who served a purpose. Not one who became…something to him. He had made a life out of *risks*—in business, in his personal life—but Francesca had swept in and made every risk feel like…life-and-death.

Aristide scowled at the dog, whose tail wagged happily. He gave one last tug before he was determined to give up. "Would you *please*…" It was as if *please* was the magic word—reminding him of too magical a night he'd turned into a disaster—that got the dog moving. It leaped up and began to run forward toward the castle. So quickly and with such force that it nearly jerked the leash out of Aristide's hand.

He managed to hold on and jog after the dog, but of course when he tried to finagle the dog inside, it only balked—and barked incessantly at the elaborate statue of a dragon that guarded this side door.

Aristide tried to use *please* again, though it rankled. Even more so when it didn't work this time. Eventually, he grabbed the dog—though it was large and heavy—and picked it up and carried it inside.

By the time he was all the way inside, and put the dog down on the ground, he was mussed and sweaty and so angry he believed he might actually storm up to her room and toss that dog in there so *she* could deal with what he'd assumed was a very *thoughtful* gift that she apparently hated him for.

Grumbling as he tried to coax the dog toward the stairs, he heard voices from the front foyer.

His mother's voice.

"You have wasted my entire evening away," he muttered at the dog. Well, they were inside now. He dropped the leash. If the dog made a mess, *Francesca* could deal with it. And now he didn't have time to fetch her for dinner.

Not that he was certain she would come.

He strode to the foyer where Vera was ushering Ginevra inside.

"Mother," he greeted stiffly, running a hand through his hair when she looked at it quizzically. No doubt a mess thanks to that monster.

Which had happily followed him and now sat obediently at his feet, like it had been doing what he ordered all evening.

Ginevra's eyes lit up and she dropped to her knees without so much as a hello to him. "A dog." She sighed as though she were in heaven, ruffling her hands over the dog's immense body as it pranced over to her. "It is my one regret, that your father is so against pets in his home. I'd love a dog or a cat or something to need me."

One regret. In this horrible life she'd chosen, the lack of a *pet* was her *one* regret.

"You could move out." Because why should she—who had kept it for over thirty years, more than half her life—consider it *his* home where she could not be allowed what *she* wanted? Why did she settle for so little when she could have everything?

She waved this away. As she always did. She got back

to her feet then looked around. "Where is your wife? Have you already scared her off?"

Aristide tried to resist a scowl, but it was impossible. As though it was *only a matter of time* before he scared her off. When Francesca had created this strange little mess they found themselves in. Because *he* had been clear.

She had pushed.

"She...is not feeling well. She will join us if she... improves." After all, Francesca lied easily and at every turn for their audiences, so why couldn't he?

"She didn't seem easily scared when I met her, but that was when she was planning to marry your brother, of course. All these stories about love whizzing about have your father in a tizzy, but I think it's sweet."

But Aristide could only focus on the first part of what she'd said. "You've met Francesca."

"Of course. When Vale brought her over to introduce her to your father."

She'd *waited* on them. He didn't know why that felt like some kind of blow. Why hadn't Francesca mentioned it? Had she not realized the woman pouring tea was his mother? Had she realized and not wanted to bring it up because she knew how he'd feel about that?

He hated to admit it, but the latter seemed far more plausible. Francesca knew the players in any room she entered. She was brilliant that way.

"I was a bit concerned you were doing this just to start trouble with your brother, but I saw a picture of you two. Some picnic. You looked happy." She reached forward, touched his cheek. "It has been a long time

since I've seen you happy, and you do not look it today.
So, why don't we sit down to dinner and you can tell
me how you've messed it up already."

She'd taken him by the arm and was leading him toward the dining room. She didn't often venture over to
his side of the island where his father was *not* welcome
and refused to come anyway. Aristide had to assume the
only reason she had this evening was because of his *wife*.

Who apparently hated him.

"She is…unhappy with me, I suppose. But it is hardly
a mess and certainly nothing I can't handle," he insisted,
pulling out a chair for her at the table.

She settled into it and waited until he took his seat.
Then she leveled him with one of her motherly glares.

"You must tell her how much you need her."

"I beg your pardon." Was he that transparent?

"You are too independent. You never let anyone know
you need them. What's a woman to do if she can't be
needed?"

Not transparent, no. Just… "A woman could be her
own person," Aristide suggested through clenched teeth.
All he'd wanted for his mother was that, and she never
taken any opportunity he'd given her.

Ginevra rolled her eyes. "I know you have no use
for me, but you must have some use for your wife, and
she must know it. If she knew it, she would meet your
mother. Not hide in her room."

No use. There had been so many "uses" he'd had for
his mother, but someone *else* had always come first. "I
needed you," he said.

She laughed, and he wished he'd kept his mouth shut.

"You made very clear you did not. Even Valentino was a better student in my kitchens than you were. He listened. You resented."

"He had his own mother."

"And so do you."

He liked to blame his father, but maybe *this* was why his mother rarely trekked out this way. They had the same circular conversations *every* time. And still he couldn't help himself, because he couldn't understand her. "I have... I have tried to give you everything."

"No, you have tried to give me what *you* want for me. But I don't want a house alone somewhere. I want to be with your father. He needs me. What would I do if I was not taking care of him? Certainly not take care of *you*. You wouldn't allow it."

"Why can't you simply take care of *yourself*? Or no one at all and just enjoy your life?"

She looked at him as if the question didn't even make sense. "What would there be to enjoy?"

Aristide shook his head. Perhaps he could just never understand her. Or Milo. Or Valentino. Or his own damn wife. Perhaps he was so alien he could not make sense of any of the people in his orbit.

Of course, there'd been a time when he'd thought he understood Francesca. Before they'd slept together. No. Before he'd told her it would not happen again. Before he'd told her...

"You love her, don't you?"

He hated the gentle, *knowing* way his mother said that. Because the way she loved his father disturbed him and he wanted nothing to do with it. "Love is a parasite," he returned, but that only made him think of Francesca.

He did not want her to need him. He did not want to need her. He did not like the version of love his mother explained to him. But there was *something* sharp and painful inside of him when it came to Francesca. Maybe his own version of a parasite.

His mother smiled indulgently. "That's not an answer to my question, Aristide."

CHAPTER THIRTEEN

FRANCESCA REFUSED TO leave her suite for three days. Even when she was tempted. Tempted to see if the dog was still around. Tempted to go for a swim. Tempted to ask Aristide why they were *here* if he wasn't making her go to some dinner or function, if he wasn't insisting she meet his mother again—because she'd been all set to refuse everything he'd asked, and then he'd gone and not asked for anything.

She focused on wallowing. Sleeping, eating whatever she wanted, drinking however much she wanted, and barely leaving her bed. She was bored and restless by day two, so she'd tried to read.

When she'd arrived at the great love confession in her book, so sweet it made her cry great wracking sobs, she'd ripped out every single page of the confession and tossed them into the fireplace, watching each lying word burn.

It had made her feel better for about five seconds.

Burning fiction didn't solve her reality.

And that was the realization she'd come to finally, which had her showering, getting dressed, and leaving her room. She'd had the sulk she'd never been allowed growing up, but that didn't change the reality.

She had to face it and determine what she wanted to do about it. She might have her freedom, but she was not completely devoid of *responsibility*.

She was so *angry* at Aristide, for so many reasons, but she had also made a mistake. He had not been wrong about her. In her taste of freedom, she had thought only of what she wanted. She had maneuvered him into what *she* wanted, because that was how she was used to surviving.

This wasn't survival anymore. It was just life. So she owed Aristide an apology. Regardless of whether he owed her one too. Regardless of whether he would offer it. An apology would not solve or change anything. That morning after back in Nice had…broken something inside of her that she did not think she could ever repair.

But perhaps they could find some common ground. A space to create two separate lives for most of the year. After all, it seemed like they'd mostly fooled the press. Maybe Aristide wasn't yet viewed as a paragon of virtue, but that would take time. As long as they stayed married and he stayed out of trouble, it should be an eventuality that came sooner rather than later.

That had been the plan anyway. Not chemistry. Not sex. Not love—that fairy tale, that *parasite* as Aristide had called it. And it was all those things, surely, if it made her feel like *this*.

She decided to take a walk on the beach to plan out what she would say to him, but the moment she stepped onto the sand she saw him in the distance. His back was to her, but he stood there on the beach, shirtless, dark swim trunks low on his hips. His hair was wet.

In front of him was the dog he'd allegedly bought her as a present.

"Stay," he ordered the dog. "Please."

At the *please* the dog went from a sitting position to a lying one. Aristide slowly began to back away from the dog—whose tail wagged harder and harder. The dog began to whimper, but it stayed.

At a certain point, Aristide stopped walking away from the dog. He turned a little, though she didn't think he'd seen her yet, but she could see his profile. A smile curved his lips. Something sharp and painful settled in her heart. A longing so deep her eyes filled with tears.

"Come," he ordered the dog and the dog leaped to its feet and bounded for him. He knelt in the sand and caught the dog's happy approach, running large hands over the dog and praising it for being a good boy.

Francesca stood frozen, watching the whole tableau play out. And she realized then and there what the real problem was. Because she had spent lifetimes convincing herself of fictions to get through the day. Finding dreams to reach for so she didn't get mired in the realities of her present.

But this was no fiction or dream. It was simply what she felt. Somewhere along the way, she'd fallen in love with him. Not just lust, not just interest, but actual love. That was the terrible choking feeling that kept taking up residence in her lungs.

That first week, he'd given her something no one ever had. And that had opened something inside of her. Not just a chance to look and enjoy her own wants and de-sires, but a chance to see herself as a free adult human being.

And in doing so, she'd seen him as an adult human being. Who was kind, and messed up, yes, but strong and solid and noble, whether he believed it about him-self or not.

So she'd fallen in love with him—foolish, parasite—it didn't matter. That was the feeling in her chest, and it would always be there. Causing her pain.

Because she knew, even if he ever fell in love in re-turn, he would only view it as the enemy. As the *para-site*. There were no happy endings for her. There never had been.

But she could find a *good* ending nonetheless. A solid one. She would find it, even in the midst of this swirl-ing realization, because she would not find herself in another prison. She would make the best of her reality. Always.

He turned suddenly, as if he'd sensed her there. But he must have heard something or seen her out of the corner of his eye.

For long, ticking seconds they only stared at each other. Across the expanse of a beach. She wanted to run to him. She wanted to run away. And she did neither.

Eventually, he walked to her, the dog staying put as if he'd given it an order to stay. When he finally ap-proached, he surveyed her outfit. Casual pants, sneak-ers and a T-shirt.

"You are not dressed to swim," he observed.

Francesca looked out at the waves lapping against

the beach. "No, I don't feel much like swimming." All those things she'd found joy in felt tainted now. Maybe that feeling would fade, but for now she had no interest in throwing herself into the waves. Because it felt like that was something *he'd* given to her.

Kindness, then cruelty. The swims, the cooking lessons, the dog whimpering off in the distance clearly wanting the go-ahead to run to them. She could not make sense of him. "Why are you so…determined to give me things I want? When it is quite clear you don't want *me*." She had to account for the heat in his gaze. "At least, you don't *want* to want me."

He was very quiet for a while, but she didn't move. Didn't take the question back. When he spoke, his voice was low.

"I needed a certain kind of wife. And wives being people aren't simply tools that one can use and discard in a closet."

"Hmm." There was that kindness again, but it wasn't about *her*, was it? "So, it is a kind of payment." Which felt…depressing. That he'd offered her things, that he'd listened and made her feel heard, only as some kind of payment.

His eyebrows drew together. "I suppose." But she could tell the way he agreed reluctantly that he didn't *actually* agree.

It didn't matter. She had things to say, and although she wasn't as prepared as she'd liked to be to say them, she needed to get it done. She met his gaze, chin raised, as if she was going to battle.

Because it felt like she was.

"I'd like to stay here while you go to London. We can pare back our outings at this point, I believe. You can focus on business. It is the natural progression of a marriage. Perhaps I'll find some sort of charitable endeavor to focus on so it seems as if I have work too. Should a large event come up, I will of course attend. If we need to be seen together, we will."

He did not say anything. He studied her with a faintly puzzled frown. So she kept talking. She needed to get it all out.

"And I would like to apologize."

The puzzled frown turned into an all-out confused scowl. "For what?"

"I should not have…pushed. *Maneuvered* you, as you said. We do not have to be at odds anymore. You were right. I will keep my distance and this will go back to what it was meant to be. A business deal. Your reputation. My freedom. Two separate, safe, content entities working together on occasion."

She forced her mouth to curve pleasantly, even though she felt positively dead inside. "So, I will leave you to your morning." She marched past him, toward the dog. "And I'll collect my present. Come," she instructed to the dog, who immediately raced up to her, then pranced about her feet as she walked resolutely down the beach.

She didn't have a destination in mind. She'd just keep marching until the threat of tears was gone.

The dog, naturally, followed her command without a second of concern for him and with none of the disobedience it had shown Aristide the past few days. Only making *some* progress today.

Well, he supposed the obedience was because of him. She could thank him later.

When? When she doesn't go to London with you?

And he was left standing on the beach as though a bomb had just detonated in his chest while her and the dog's form got smaller and smaller.

When, really, this was ideal. Time apart would be good for them. No doubt with some space they could get back to how it had been in the beginning, as she'd suggested. An easy kind of…friendship wasn't the right word. She'd said business deal, but he didn't love that phrase either.

Well, it didn't matter what they called it. Everything was back on clear, even ground where they belonged.

But she didn't come to lunch or dinner that night, even though he'd sent a staff member to fetch her. They'd returned, looking uncomfortable, with news that Francesca preferred to eat in her room as the dog would no doubt misbehave in the dining room.

The following day, he'd hoped he might catch her for a walk on the beach—she'd taken over the care of the dog, so certainly he'd have to run into her outside at some point.

But he never did.

Knowing she was here had been one thing when he'd thought she was angry with him. He was used to anger. To being shut out because he had disappointed or hurt someone. Everything he'd done during those first three days they'd been here had been *at* that anger. Take care of her idiot dog, work as though he was not upset or pre occupied, dine with his mother and such. He'd done it to prove her anger had no sway over him.

And he'd felt all of thirteen, existing in the icy silences of Valentino's determination that there was nothing more between them now that they shared a terrible father.

But now he knew she wasn't angry, or at least said she wasn't, and he didn't know what to do with the tired way she'd come to him with a truce of sorts. How she'd *apologized*. How he was supposed to feel as settled as though they were on the same page, when it seemed she was still avoiding him.

Well, he did not have to be avoided in his own home. He did not have to use his staff as *messengers*. He stood, forgetting his half-eaten dinner and strode across the castle to her suite of rooms. He knocked on her main door—with probably more force than necessary—and warned himself to get his strange, confusing, tempestuous feelings under control.

He would not take them out on her. That was not who he was. And he didn't *need* her. To be his dinner companion. To *need* to be his. *Need* had no place here.

This clawing feeling inside of him wasn't any of the things his mother had talked about. No. They were just needing this settled, when clearly if she was avoiding him, *she* was not settled.

Francesca opened her suite door, a careful look on her face. He thought she was trying to look placid, but he saw the trepidation and suspicion in her dark gaze.

She had opened the door wide, but she still held on

to it, like it might be needed to shut it in his face. The dog was curled up by the unnecessary fire in the hearth.

Everything about the scene was cozy, down to what she wore. Despite the fact fall was on the way, it still felt like summer, but she was dressed in soft, fuzzy material meant for lounging. She looked so…soft. Infinitely touchable.

He shoved his hands in his pockets. *He* was the one who'd drawn that line, had he not? "I came to tell you I am going to London in the morning," he said stiffly.

She smiled, with absolutely no warmth. "Excellent. I hope you have a wonderful trip."

"I'd like you to join me at the end of the week to attend a fundraiser."

She nodded, still gripping the door. "Naturally."

That should be it. Their staff would handle the arrangements and he would see her again in London at the end of the week.

"Have you ever been to the National Gallery?" he asked.

"Well, no."

"We can go together the following day." They should do more than events, after all. Keep the stories about them.

"For a photo op?" she asked, carefully.

Yes, that was what he'd been thinking. He should nod and agree. But something about the scene in front of him had him…wanting to be a part of it. "It does not have to be."

"Then I would not want to intrude on your schedule." She smiled blandly at him. Like she had in those first moments he'd stolen her away from Vale. She'd held her own but kept herself carefully under wraps. "I'm sure I can handle a visit on my own."

"It does not suit our image if you're wandering about the museum without my company."

She nodded thoughtfully at that. "Well, perhaps another time, then."

Because she'd rather not go than be with him at all. After…making amends. After apologizing to him. She made no earthly sense. And it should make him angry. He was angry.

That was the twisting, clawing feeling inside of him. Anger, not panic. Control, not loss.

"Was there anything else?" she asked, sounding vaguely curious when he could see exactly what she wanted in her eyes. She wanted him to leave.

Leave.

"Breakfast. We will eat a meal together before I go." He did not dress it up as a question, because it was an order.

She looked back at her *dog*, lolling in front of the fire like some kind of boneless creature with fur. "Liborio is still learning his table manners." She returned her gaze to him with that fake mask of a smile. "Perhaps when you return."

It was not a real excuse. The dog didn't *need* to eat with them. And he could have pointed that out. Might have, if there was not some hint of vulnerability underneath that mask she'd once worn so well.

But he could see under it now. He could see *her* now.

"Is that disastrous dog really deserving of such a name?"

For a moment, just the smallest, quickest moment, he saw the flash of temper in her eyes. One he would have welcomed in the here and now, because it was more like...before. When they had enjoyed each other's company. Before everything had been complicated by crossing *lines*—just like he'd known everything would be.

Without answering his question, she stepped back, and didn't meet his gaze. "Good night, Aristide."

And she closed the door. Gently. But in his face all the same.

CHAPTER FOURTEEN

WITH ARISTIDE GONE to London, Francesca put herself to work. Mostly on training Liborio, who was indeed a bit of a disaster. But a wonderful one. He gave her a purpose and company. She didn't feel quite so lonely with Liborio in tow.

Mostly.

But she refused to think about what the castle felt like without Aristide's presence in it. Empty and like all the color was muted. She focused on a list of to-dos she curated for herself instead.

She went through Aristide's charitable endeavors. The ones he kept quiet. Looking for an idea of how she might spend her now ample free time. She had always managed her father's life, but Aristide had a staff in place for that. Perhaps she should take over some of it, but right now she still felt too raw to insert herself into his plans.

No, she'd find something for herself. Perhaps she could throw her own version of a fundraiser here for one of the organizations he'd donated to. Before she could really dig into a plan, though, she was interrupted by a staff member entering the room.

"Signora Bonaparte. There is a phone call for you."

She blinked once at Luca. She was almost used to being called Bonaparte now, but it was the idea that someone was calling the house to talk to her that made her feel…out of place. She couldn't think of a single person who would do so rather than call her mobile.

Except…perhaps Aristide. The way her heart leaped at the thought was downright *depressing*. And still, she reached for the phone with a terrible bubble of hope in her throat that she didn't want.

She didn't want him or love or hope. She wanted her old certainty back. Her old purpose back. Somehow, Aristide had taken that away from her and she didn't know what to *do*.

Blowing out an irritated breath, she held the phone to her ear. "Hello?"

"Buon giorno, Francesca. This is Ginevra. Aristide's mother."

"Oh." She tried to find something to say to that, but she didn't know why Aristide's mother would be calling her when Francesca hadn't even shown up to the dinner they'd had a few nights ago.

"I thought perhaps if you weren't busy this afternoon, you could come to tea. I have an open afternoon and would love to get to know you."

Again, the only thing Francesca could think to say was, "Oh."

"And bring your dog, if you'd like."

She looked down at Liborio, who was on his back, wriggling around, as if trying to reach some itch. "I…" She didn't want to go over there. Maybe she should claim illness again.

"See you at two, then," Ginevra said cheerfully, and then the line went dead.

Ending any possibility of refusing. Francesca stared at the phone in her hand for some time before it penetrated that she needed to hang up the phone. Probably fix her makeup a bit. Find Liborio's leash. If they left now, they could walk over to the main Bonaparte estate and arrive on time.

So, that was what she did. Hoping the walk would settle her some, give her some ideas on how to talk to Ginevra. Regardless of her feelings for Aristide, she was married to him for the long haul. She wanted to be… well, not his friend. That hurt too much. But a separate partner, and that certainly meant being on his mother's good side would be a positive.

She set out across the island, chastising the eager dog for pulling on his leash. Summer's heat had lifted, and though when it was sunny it could still be quite warm, fall was making its way onto the island.

When she arrived at the titular Bonaparte residence, she did not feel any affinity for the classically beautiful and historic estate. It felt…cold. A defiant slap of man against the wild, instead of Aristide's artistic, wild partnership with it.

Which was neither here nor there. She picked her way up the yard to the main entrance. The door was wide open, and a woman stood there. Liborio immediately started yipping happily but Francesca kept a firm grip on the leash.

She needed *something* to grip on to. She plastered an old, polite smile on her face as she approached Aristide's mother. "Good afternoon…" She trailed off because she realized the woman wouldn't have the last name Bonaparte, so she did not know how to address her.

But the woman smiled all the same. "It is good to see you again, Francesca. Please, don't hesitate to call me Ginevra." She looked warmly from Francesca to Liborio's wriggling body.

"I heard Aristide was in London and you'd stayed behind. Perhaps I should have waited for him to return, but it seemed like the perfect time to meet my daughter-in-law without my son to color the meeting." She knelt down to meet Liborio's incessant barks. "And to see this one again." She scrubbed her hands over his fur. "He is a prize."

"Aristide…picked him out."

Ginevra leaned back on her heels, looked up at Francesca speculatively. "Fascinating." Then she straightened. "Well, come. Follow me inside. Milo is on the mainland, and a woman can only polish the sconces so many times, even in a house such as this. So it seemed the perfect day for an elaborate tea and some company."

"I can tie Liborio outside if—"

"Nonsense. Bring him in. Liborio. What a clever name."

Francesca followed her inside. A grand foyer, an even grander main room. All dark woods and what must be ancient art and furniture, very well-tended but…dark. Stuffy. Overbearing. Until they moved into a small room off the kitchen. A sort of breakfast nook. Bright and colorful. Whimsical enough to remind her of Aristide.

He had spoken of his mother's love for his father

in terrible terms like *parasite*. Vale, if he'd deigned to speak about his father—never his mother—had been much the same. And it made no sense to Francesca either, that all this light and color would stay amid all that dark.

"Sit. Sit. Nothing formal." Ginevra smiled, pointing at a table already piled high with tiny sandwiches and cakes and a pretty, floral teapot.

Francesca took a seat, quietly ordered Liborio to sit—which he thankfully did, panting up at the two women happily.

"I was sorry to have missed you the other evening," Francesca said as Ginevra poured. "I wasn't feeling quite up to it."

"You and Aristide were having a fight. I wouldn't want to sit at a dinner with anyone either in that situation."

Francesca opened her mouth to argue, even if it would have been a lie, but she saw a knowing kind of look on Ginevra's face. Had Aristide *told* his mother they were fighting?

"I couldn't get the whole truth out of him, of course," Ginevra continued with an easy wave of the hand. Everything about her was so...*effortless*. "He hasn't told me a whole truth since he was thirteen."

Thirteen. Yes, she supposed a lot of Aristide had changed at that moment. Finding out his real father, somehow gaining and losing a brother in one fell swoop.

"Though this time it wasn't so much that he didn't want to tell me what was wrong, it was more he could not seem to figure out what he did wrong."

"He didn't do anything wrong." Francesca looked down at her hands. How awkward this all was.

"Ah, I do not wish to make you uncomfortable, if you don't want to discuss it. I just know how…contained Aristide can be. And how isolated this island can be. I wanted you to know, you can view me as a friend. And I happen to be a friend who…well, I don't know that I *understand* my son, but I see him better than most. So many don't see the real him because he can put on a show. Like his father."

Ginevra was about the only person Francesca thought she'd seen smile when mentioning the feared Milo Bonaparte.

"Having met…all of you now, I think Aristide takes after you more than Mr. Bonaparte."

Ginevra cocked her head and studied her as she piled two plates high with all manner of treats. She put one in front of Francesca, and one in front of herself, then tossed a little piece of biscuit to Liborio.

"I doubt he would agree with you, but I am glad to hear it. I've always thought so myself, but Aristide is good at…masks." Ginevra took a hefty bite of a sandwich, then chewed thoughtfully. Her gaze seemed to flit about the pretty room, the dog, but then zeroed in on Francesca.

"And so are you. You're not quite like how I remember you when you were with Vale."

Francesca didn't know what to say. Ginevra didn't say it scathingly or accusingly, but it was still…touchy. She had jumped from marrying one brother to another. In one day.

"Vale was never mine, of course, but I cared for both boys. As best I could. I'm not holding moving from one to another against you. I know how easy it is for people to look at a situation and judge it. *I* am a judgment-free zone."

Francesca did not know this woman well enough to tell her the truth. That it was hard to be judged when she had been willing to marry either brother for those mercenary reasons that seemed so far away now, even though just over a month ago she'd still been under her father's thumb.

She should be happy, really, that her problems now were not being worried about life and limb. Just the state of her foolish heart.

"You know, dining with my son earlier this week reminded me of when he was younger. When he and Vale had their falling out. He is very good at *reacting*, but not always so good at understanding."

Francesca didn't laugh exactly, but it verbalized what she felt about trying to get through to Aristide. He had all his lines, all his ideas, and in his mind everything had to follow. If it didn't, he didn't find out why. He simply…shut it down.

"But I suppose that is our relationship. A lack of understanding. He does not understand why I stay. What being needed means to me. We don't understand each other, I suppose, since he has made certain to build a life where no one needs him, and he is not needed anywhere. That makes *me* sad, but perhaps it makes him happy." Ginevra reached across the table and took Francesca's hands. "I would so like it if you could make him happy."

Francesca looked into the woman's warm, dark eyes. "By…needing him?"

Ginevra nodded.

But it landed in Francesca all wrong. It wasn't *need* she felt. Need was not…a choice. Need made it sound like an addiction, a cure to a disease. This horrible feeling inside of her that ate her up wasn't need, because she could live without it. She would happily live without it.

It wasn't that she *needed* him. It was that she wanted him. To do nice things for her, while she took care of him. She wanted some semblance of…connecting. She did not want to be stuck in a mausoleum, waiting on him, all to feel needed.

No, she understood Aristide's position on his mother, because she knew Milo. She wouldn't judge Ginevra. Perhaps there was something in the odious man that worked for her, but Francesca could not call it love.

It reminded her too much of her father's control. A man who would continue to treat the woman he'd fathered a child with as an *employee*. Who allowed her to have no say, no visibility in his life. This was not a man in love.

"I don't need Aristide, and he doesn't need me," Francesca said gently, hoping to explain it in a way that might make sense to Ginevra. "I think…we have made great mistakes with each other on a personal level, but we can be… Well, our relationship won't be about love or need. It's more a…partnership."

Ginevra studied her for a long while, still holding Francesca's hands. "Forgiveness of mistakes is a choice."

Francesca didn't doubt it, but she could not continue

to forgive someone for the same thing for thirty years. She couldn't hide herself hoping for a crumb or a morsel of need. No, this was not the life she wanted for herself, regardless of Aristide.

"I think...love might be too." She thought about the *before*, when she'd been falling in love with Aristide. Perhaps she could have stopped it, but she hadn't because loving him opened up a lifetime of wonderful possibilities.

For him, it wasn't that he did not have some feeling for her, it was that he did not like the possibilities her love offered.

So, they had chosen. And that was that.

She changed the subject to dogs, to the weather, to the decor in this room. They had a lovely little tea and spoke of superficial topics from that point on. Still, it was nice. It didn't feel like a performance so much as the layers to a possible friendship. Sometimes serious, sometimes not.

When she got up, she allowed Ginevra to hug her. And when she said, "Thank you," she meant it.

Ginevra pulled back, held Francesca by the elbows. "I always dreamed of a daughter. It would be my great pleasure if this could become a weekly occurrence for us. Regardless of love and Aristide and Milo, I would like to be friends with you, Francesca." She smiled.

A lump clogged Francesca's throat. To think she could be friends with someone at all, let alone when they didn't agree, felt like...an epiphany. "I'd like that." She looked down at Liborio's happy panting. "He would too."

"Excellent. We will consider it a date."

* * *

Aristide paced the main room in his modern London apartment. He'd purchased it as a direct contrast to Valentino's staid, upstanding home here. He had wanted to highlight those differences, always. It had felt like *proving* something.

But he realized starkly in this moment as he waited for Francesca, tied up over Francesca, *desperate and aching* over that woman, that every petty little thing he'd done in the past twenty years *at* his brother had only been this.

Trying to get his attention. Because he didn't have the words, didn't know how to tell Valentino what he wanted—a brother, a relationship, some reparation now that he had almost fully eradicated Milo from his life.

So, unlike his castle back on the island that he had built *mostly* for himself, and only a *little* at Valentino and Milo, this ugly, empty, monstrosity of an apartment brought him no joy.

He wanted to turn his anger at this to Francesca. How would he have realized these gestures were so pathetic and empty if she hadn't accused him of hiding his wants?

So all this pain, this upheaval, this *emptiness* was her fault and she wasn't *here*.

She had agreed to come, and they would need to leave for the event soon. So not only was she at fault for the roiling disarray inside of him, but she was *late*. It stoked his temper even higher.

Surely it was *temper*, not fear. What did he have to be afraid of?

He heard voices in the foyer, and then Francesca *finally* appeared. She smiled at him, that bland, heiress smile from *before*. She was already dressed for the fundraising event. A simple black dress, not going too far toward staid matron, but not quite the sparkly purple contraption that still haunted his dreams.

"Are you ready to go?" she asked by way of greeting.

"No dog in tow?" he asked, and he knew it sounded like a growl, like an accusation. He did not know what to do to stop it. Because *she* was the only one who ever stripped away his control.

She was the problem.

"Your mother was kind enough to offer to watch him. She's quite fond of him."

"My mother."

"Yes. We had tea yesterday. I quite like her." The fake smile warmed a degree. "I think you take after her more than you'd like to admit."

She said this like a compliment when it was the *worst* thing that she could have said to him. Was this awful, roiling thing inside of him what his mother felt for Milo? Was this the *need* she spoke of that made her put a terrible, horrible man above all else?

But Francesca isn't terrible. He didn't know where that voice in his head came from. He could only stare at her, terrified she had ruined him irreparably.

"What have you done to me?" he demanded, at his wits' end. Because he did not recognize this version of himself. The kind that couldn't let go. He had always set people aside. Built an armor that kept *out* anyone who wanted in.

He did not *need*. He was not a glutton for punishment. He did not demand to be in the orbit of people who didn't want him.

Because no one does.

His chest felt tight. He wanted to believe that very clear message life had taught him, but she kept being here, kept...hurting him by simply existing. And he did not know how to permanently set her aside. He kept *wanting* her.

And it felt so uncomfortably like the *need* his mother spoke of, he wanted to rip this apartment down to the studs with his two bare hands.

Her eyebrows had gone up and she studied him with that detached way she had with *other* people. She wasn't supposed to have it with him. Why could *she* control this?

"I don't understand what you mean," she said, carefully enunciating each word.

But neither did he. He didn't understand *any* of this.

Except he wanted his hands on her. He wanted to forget his lines ever existed. He wanted to watch her swim and take her to bed and bring her a million gifts so she would smile at him like she had when he'd tasted her first cake.

"What you want could matter if you would tell me," she had said to him. Naked in his bed. Hurt, from the words and accusations he'd hurled at her.

But how did he tell her what he wanted? When that seemed to ensure he would never, ever have it?

"If we plan it out, we could have a child," he said, and he *heard* his own desperation, the beat of panic at offering such a ridiculous thing. But this would work… It would have to work. She'd been so upset about not being pregnant, and even if she should have been relieved, she hadn't been. She wanted a child and… And…and…

Much like with the dog, this did not have the desired effect. She did not look happy or excited. She didn't even look detached anymore. She looked furious.

"Oh, could we?"

And sounded more so.

"I am trying to give you what you want," he ground out, wondering why she had to make that so damn difficult. Why he couldn't make her respond the way she was *supposed* to.

She shook her head. "No. I don't know what you're trying to do, but throwing *gifts* at me as if I'm supposed to be constantly grateful to you is… It has to stop. Now, we should go or we will be late and people will talk."

"I do not want to go."

She rolled her eyes at him. "Ah. What would *you* like to do then, Aristide? Or can you find the words to say even that?"

"I want…" Something was crashing inside of him, crumbling into nothing but dust. His very bones perhaps. What did he want? Not this. Not this crushing. Not this *need* that would destroy him and her.

He wasn't sure he could *breathe*. Something in her expression changed like she could see that. Some of her anger softened. "Perhaps I was wrong," she said quietly. "I assumed you kept what you want hidden, but maybe you truly don't even know what you want."

I want you. I want you. I want you.

But he couldn't say that. If he did… If he did…

"I find that sad, but I am slowly realizing what *I* want in the wake of all this, and it isn't…what we're doing. It isn't misery and shouting matches and…whatever this is."

"What are you saying?"

"We should take some time apart. Really apart. If people begin to talk, we'll come up with a story. But I think we need some time away for the dust to settle."

"No."

"Aristide."

She sounded so *tired*, so *resigned*. When she was the one who'd upended *his* life. "You did this."

She shook her head. "No. No. I'm not doing this." She whirled around, ready to march out of the room no doubt, but he grabbed her arm.

And found absolutely no words when she glared at him.

"How about this, Aristide. Maybe *this* will get through to you." She sucked in a breath and let it out and continued with words that made absolutely no sense. "I love you."

It was like being lanced clean through. A sharp, unbearable pain. He thought perhaps he'd even stumbled back, but he wasn't sure he could feel his body.

"And I know you do not want that. *I* don't even want it. But I cannot seem to make it go away. So being near you hurts. And I will not put myself through any *hurt* just because…" She waved a hand at him. "I want… more. I rather enjoy—or at least enjoyed—your company. Perhaps I pushed too hard too fast at that first taste of freedom, but I like working together. I like you. What I want is not a child or a dog plopped down in the absence of feeling. I don't want *needs* overriding choice. I want a life."

Life. Every time he'd hoped for *life*—a brother, a father, a mother who put him above the man who *needed* her, he had been rebuffed. So he had built a life that demanded nothing of him. Because that was all he was meant for. "I cannot give that to you, Francesca."

"I didn't ask you to. I told you what I wanted. You have given me much, Aristide, but I never asked any of it *from* you. You saw it, decided to give it. All on your own."

"I don't know what you're talking about." Because that made it sound like…he'd done it on purpose when it was just…

She laughed. Bitterly. "No. Baking lessons and ridiculous dogs were certainly not *your* choices. You go out of your way to make everyone in your path happy."

If only that were true. But he could not think of a single person in his path who was *happy*. "You don't seem happy."

"No, but that is *me*, Aristide. I am not happy because no amount of *things* you throw at me can change the fact that I want more. Like I said. A *life*."

He did not mean to say the words in his head. He'd meant to keep them to himself. "I don't have that in me."

For a moment, when he caught just a flash on her face of some kind of sympathy, he thought it might be all right. She'd feel sorry for him enough to *stop* this. Or to fix it, somehow. She with her plans and her strength, she could fix it.

But it was only a flash.

"Do you not have it in you, or are you afraid that it will be difficult? That you will make mistakes? That we will fight and feel things that hurt?" She shook her head, and tears were filling her eyes but they didn't fall. "Aristide, we are not our parents. We are not simply *pain* dressed up in skin. We get to decide these things. What we want. What we love. What we stand for. But you are afraid to open your eyes."

And she said that with such dismissiveness, more words he didn't mean to say poured out. "I am *afraid* that I will destroy you."

Like I destroy all relationships.

He never meant to. They just all crumbled in his hands.

"Because once upon a time your brother could not handle the truth?" she demanded, somehow seeing through him when he barely saw through himself. "A truth neither of you have ever once addressed in nearly twenty years. Because you do not understand your mother and she does not understand you? What other relationship have you ever attempted?"

He wanted to find some way to stop her. Stop *this*, but she just kept talking. Each word a sharp stab of pain. Of truth.

"None, is the answer, Aristide. Something painful happened to you at thirteen, and you shut yourself off from all other painful things. Because you had the *lux-ury* to do so. Well, I never had that choice, so I guess

I never learned how to deal with them like an adult."
She shook her head. "Maybe love itself is not a choice,
but doing something about it is, and we have made our
choices."

She kept saying *love*, like it did nothing but backfire.
Disappoint. *Hurt.*

"Actually, I take that back. *I* have made my choice.
Per usual, you have let all the choices of others fall on
your shoulders so you can disengage and blame someone else. If you want me, Aristide, if you love me, you
will have to *choose*. I cannot do it for you, and even if
I could, I wouldn't. Give the hosts my apologies. I cannot be near you right now. I cannot...*do this* with you
anymore."

And as quickly as she'd arrived, she left, and somehow, he felt worse.

Worst of all, for the first time in his life, he had no
one to blame but himself.

Which meant, he was the only one who could fix this.
The only one who could...lay himself bare. Say what he
wanted. Like she had done.

And trust that his angel, his life, his *love* was strong
enough to handle it.

CHAPTER FIFTEEN

FRANCESCA DID NOT know where to go. She only knew that she *had* to go.

"If we plan it out, we could have a child."

How could he hurt her so much without even meaning to? Because for all his faults, she knew there had been something genuine in that offer. Not about having a child but giving her something he thought would make her happy. He hadn't meant for it to hurt.

And she wanted it so badly, it nearly cut her in two. But she couldn't stand the idea of sobbing in front of him right now. She needed to make this stand. They could not keep hurting each other if he was not willing to *grow*. To be brave.

She had not been to Aristide's London apartment before, and she did not know her way around. She should march back out the front door, but one of the staff members had taken her things and put them somewhere. She at least needed her purse so she needed to find...someone to tell her where to go.

But the apartment seemed deserted, and every room she stuck her head into offered little help, until she came across the strangest thing. A wall of glass, and on the other side of it…a pool.

So surprised by this, she went for the door. When she stepped inside, the air hit her, heavy and warm, like an embrace. Big potted plants were clustered in different corners of the room so that it was a bit like a tropical oasis. The pool was not large, but it was blue and flashed invitingly under the overhead lights.

She moved forward until she was standing at the edge of the pool. Somehow swimming had become the first beacon of her freedom. This wasn't the ocean, but…she just needed to do something. Act.

Feel.

She jumped in. It was foolish. Worse even than skinny-dipping as she was probably ruining her clothes. What would she do when she emerged? She had no towel, no change of clothes.

But she had found her joy in the water. In throwing herself into the waves that first week of freedom. She had felt baptized and sure and made new, and she needed *something* to make her feel that again. Even if it was the most nonsensical thing she'd ever done.

Falling in love is the most nonsensical thing you've ever done, some harsh voice in her head whispered.

And fair enough. It was certainly why she was here. When she should have known better. Should have some-how predicted he would make the most insulting, hurt-ful offer he could muster.

"If we plan it out, we could have a child."

Like it was a bargaining chip. A *bribe*. Only she

couldn't decide what he wanted from her. Not love. Not a true wife. So *what*?

He thought she'd *done* something to him, but he'd rejected her. Set her aside. Made it very clear his lines were all he wanted. And he couldn't *love*.

What rot.

She let herself submerge under the water completely. Ruining her makeup, no doubt. Her careful updo. Ruining *everything*.

She welcomed it. Never in her life had she been allowed to ruin anything without consequences, and so this was just another freedom. She resurfaced once her lungs couldn't hold any longer, making sure her hair was swept off her face as she stood again. If she was crying, she couldn't tell because she was now wet straight through.

But the ragged breath that came out of her sure sounded like a sob that echoed around the room. But after that echo there was…another sound. She looked over at the entrance to the room.

Aristide.

Looking like some sort of avenging god as he strode across the tile to the stairs into the pool. Her breath caught in her throat, even though she did not want to fight with him any longer. She didn't want *this* any longer. She wanted…

Oh, if only she knew what she wanted that didn't involve *him*.

He didn't *stop* his approach. He didn't demand she get out of the pool like Francesca expected. He walked right into the water. Suit and all. Right toward her. Strong, impatient strides like the water was nothing. "I do not like who I am when you are away," he bit out like an accusation. "I do not like who I am when we are fighting. I do not like the idea I have…hurt you."

She wanted to swim away but found herself rooted to the spot by his hot gaze and angry mouth and the fact he had not left her. He had…come after her. Like there could be change, growth. Like maybe… But his words… My God, the man was dense.

"The *idea*? You *did* hurt me. You hurt me on purpose."

He shook his head, moving closer still. "On purpose would mean I did anything *to* hurt you, but all I keep trying to do is to *save* you." He held out his hands, palms up. "Don't you *see*?"

But his hands were empty, and even though he looked anguished, she very much did *not* see. She knew she should turn away. Knew she shouldn't let him do whatever this was.

But she loved him, for good or for ill, and she did not know how to turn her back on this love even if it would save her from more hurt.

Maybe, just maybe, the hurt was worth it if love was the end result.

"I do not know how to hold the people I love without…sending them away. Without them sending *me* away," he said, each word a pained confession from deep within.

Love. Her heart leaped, even though it had no business doing so. "Do you think I would?" she managed through a voice little more than croak.

"You already have!" he all but shouted, his voice echoing with pain in the small room as water lapped around them.

"Because I didn't thank you for your pity dog or take you up on the offer for a pity child?" she demanded, wounded that he could possibly claim these things were him trying.

"It isn't pity," he growled.

"Then what is it?" she returned, wondering why she was letting this conversation happen. Why they were standing in a *pool*, for Heaven's sake.

"Penance!" he roared, loud and painful, like an admonition that had been wrenched out of him with great force and pain.

And she had no idea what to say to that, how to wrap her mind around such a thing. "Aristide. For *what*?"

"I have tried. To make it up to anyone. I tried to be as good as Valentino and I could not be—my father wouldn't let me be. I was…a tool to hurt his *real* son, at best. I have tried to get her to leave, to find her *own* life. But I could not convince her." He didn't need to say who. Francesca knew he meant his mother.

And she had known his parents pained him, but perhaps she had not fully understood the scars they'd left. Because he was very careful not to let that show. And could she blame him? Hadn't she hidden her father's abuse from *everyone*?

Everyone except him.

"As for Valentino…" he said roughly.

But he never finished his sentence. Never seemed to find the words to verbalize what he felt about his brother. Francesca couldn't help but wonder if it was because there was still some hope there. That half of his anguish was the continued hope that the family who had hurt him might change.

But while he waited, hoped, he had fashioned his life in the shadow of what they'd done to him—purposefully or not—and she understood that too well to keep her heart hardened to him.

She reached out and took his outstretched hands, still both of them standing in this warm pool with their dinner clothes on. "You cannot judge yourself on other people's choices, Aristide. Do you not think I hear my father's voice in my head sometimes? That I am worthless? That I deserve whatever hurts come my way?"

He made a noise of protest as he gripped her hands, but she continued on.

"Of course I do. Of course I feel that sometimes, but I refuse to let the harm he caused me define me or my life."

"Francesca."

But he said nothing else. Just her name as if it was pain, as he held her hands tightly in this pool. She wanted to laugh. She wanted to cry. But what they needed, she knew, was an answer.

An end, some little voice whispered at her. And maybe she would have listened to it just a few moments ago, but being reminded that *sometimes* the voice in her head was not her own, not about her best interests, she shoved it aside.

"Come. Let us…go have a rational conversation. Somewhere dry."

* * *

Aristide helped her out of the pool. He could not fathom how they had come to such a ridiculous situation. Soaked and fully dressed. It was out of control and solved nothing. How could this solve anything?

Except here she was. Touching him. Letting him dry her off. He moved the towel over her hair, her shoulders, while she watched him with those careful dark eyes.

He hated that she was careful with him. Hated when she put on that mask. And yet when she'd dropped it, that night all these weeks ago now, he'd hurt her. On purpose, he supposed, even if he'd been thinking more of saving himself than hurting her.

He had hurt her.

To save himself.

And that…cut him to shreds. On top of all the other things swirling inside of him, because even now, looking a bit like a wet poodle, she made him feel all of these things he had so carefully eradicated from his life. She made him *face* them, all because…

All because he loved her. Beyond any kind of reason he could find. That thing he'd been so careful to avoid. Love and need and the inevitable end of the things he cared for.

But the things she said…like ends were not inevitable. The things she'd been through and could still come out on the other side believing… She was good and whole and worthy. She was, of course. So good, his angel.

She couldn't really believe… Not when she was this driving force.

She had been trying to understand him, get to the

bottom of what he wanted. And she wasn't perfect. She hadn't always used good means, but she was *trying*.

What had he done? As she'd accused him, just thrown things at her that might make her happy in the hopes he would not be called upon to do so.

He blotted her face with the towel, then dropped it and let his hands cup her skin. Damp and soft. Warm and his. Oh, how he wanted her to be his. But...

"Francesca, *mio angioletta*, I am afraid that everything I feel will hurt you."

She studied him with those serious, dark eyes. A study that spoke of great contemplation. She was weighing his words, and it hurt that she did not have an immediate response, and yet this consideration made him think that whatever she said would be true and important and deep. Not just a knee-jerk reaction.

"Maybe your feelings will hurt me, but...as you said, this is not a hurt that is *meant*, that is done *at* each other. Life...hurts. Cruelty and hurt are not the same."

"Is the bar so low that not being cruel is all you expect of me?" he murmured, brushing wet strands of hair off her face.

She shook her head, her mouth almost curving. "Aristide, I have been so angry with you, so frustrated, but it wasn't until I told you *why*, directly, that anything changed. That you walked into that pool with me. Perhaps the trick is not...worrying so much about hurting one another, but being brave enough to tell each other when we are hurt, and...jump in the metaphorical pool and work it out."

"I would give you anything."

She sighed, clearly not happy with those words, but she reached out and touched her fingertips to his cheek rather than step away. "I do not need your gifts. I need you. Not in the way your mother spoke of need. I do not think that is love, because it is one-sided. Whatever she does for your father, is one-sided. Perhaps she gets something out of it, but it isn't from *him*. I need *you*."

He did not know how to give himself. Or maybe, he knew. However, he had never been rewarded for such a choice. But this was Francesca. Even amidst a fear born of a tempestuous childhood, he knew she was somehow the beacon of light through that.

And he would have to tell her, really admit it. Because trying to separate from her didn't work; it only made this pain worse. "I love you, and I worry that it will be the end of me. The end of you."

"Change doesn't always have to be bad, Aristide. I have changed my life for the better. Even jumping into that pool fully clothed, even fighting with you, even having my heart shattered, this is better."

He closed his eyes in pain. That so little could be better.

"And maybe it will be an end. An end of a you or a me that no longer serves us."

He scowled a bit at that. "You sound like my mother."

"I like your mother. I might not agree with her on everything, but she is... She loves you, Aristide."

"Yes." It was hard sometimes, because she had made choices that had valued his father over him. It was hard, because she was not perfect. She had deep, meaningful flaws.

But…perhaps the point was that he did not have to make the same mistakes. Perhaps the point was that the love Francesca offered him *was* love, and that meant…

Here she stood, saying she loved him. Trying to *reach* him. No one had ever done such a thing for him before, and he didn't want to trust it.

But he trusted Francesca. How could he not?

"Say it again," she said, her fingers in his hair. Her eyes large and luminous. And the warmth of her—body and soul—seeping into him. Yes, it turned out, he would risk anything for this, fight anything for this, even his own deep-seated fears.

"I love you, Francesca."

Her mouth curved, so beautiful. So perfect. His angel.

"I love you too, Aristide."

"Then we will build our life from here on out. On that love. On that promise. And I will learn how to be strong. From you. I promise you, Francesca, I am yours. Forever. If you will be mine."

"Forever," she whispered, and then pressed her mouth to his. A promise. Hope. All those things he thought were the enemy, but all they'd ever been were…

His for the taking. Just like her.

EPILOGUE

They returned to the island and spent the next few weeks determining how they would build this life they would share. As husband and wife. As two people who loved one another. They laid out what they wanted, and they didn't always agree, but Francesca was glad for it.

Because neither of them balked at that first fight after they'd said their *I love you*s. Oh, they'd gone to their separate corners, no doubt. Francesca had ranted to the dog while she'd taken him out on a walk. Aristides had disappeared into his gym.

And when they'd both returned home, sweaty and out of breath, they'd met there in the middle of the castle and just begun…laughing.

She knew not all arguments would be resolved so easily, so cheerfully, but some would be. It was the *life* she was after.

Just like befriending Ginevra, planning a charitable fundraising event on the island, and extending an invitation to Valentino to attend.

There'd been no response to that, but Francesca was determined, and everyone knew what happened when Francesca *determined* something.

She was gratified when Aristide stopped trying to talk her out of it, and instead made a suggestion of his own. As they were lying in bed one night. After the *very* hard work of perhaps starting their very own family.

"We are slated to go to an event in London in a few weeks. I will head to the Diamond Club. Make certain to run into Valentino there. Offer an olive branch."

"What kind of olive branch?"

"We'll think of something."

She pressed a kiss to his beautiful shoulder. "I like the sound of *we*."

In a smooth move, he easily rolled her on top of him and grinned up at her. "A we forever, *mio angioletta*."

And nothing was better than *forever*.

When they returned to London, with the express intent of making the first step of an inroad with his brother, it was with happy news. A child on the way. Not a deal, a bribe, or unplanned. A choice. Born of love.

"He may not be ready yet," Francesca said firmly as Aristide readied himself for a visit to the Diamond Club. "But you are opening a door."

They had discussed it at length, so he nodded, even if he was not sure he was ready for this. But not only would he do anything to make his wife happy, he wanted to *try* to fix what he and Valentino had broken as young men.

She gave him a squeeze at the door and he slid his hand down her abdomen as he couldn't seem to stop himself from doing multiple times a day, marveling that a child would grow there. Their child. A mix of them both and a hope for a future.

"And I will be here, even if it remains closed. Always." She rose to her toes and brushed a kiss across his mouth.

He smiled at her, his angel, and bid her goodbye so that he could make his way to the club. Much like he had in the past, he had ways of knowing when Vale was there. How and when to show up to irritate his brother.

But that wasn't the goal tonight. He would try very hard for that not to be the end result either.

He had thought little of the Diamond Club since Francesca had swept into his life—because as much as he'd been the one to steal her—she had been the one to change everything. But it remained unchanged as ever.

The clubhouse itself was on a discreet and quiet street. Like his brother, Aristide kept a suite there. The staff was almost supernaturally excellent, capable of anticipating every whim almost before it was formed.

And so, it was easy enough to find the room where his brother sat, scowling with a drink in hand. Aristide got himself a drink before he carefully made his way over to the seat on the other side of Valentino.

When Valentino looked over, he scowled. "I do not recall inviting you to sit," Valentino said after a baleful moment. "But then, you have never needed an invitation to intrude upon me, have you?"

Aristide didn't *sigh*, though it was a hard-won thing. He had learned that sometimes…relationships took work. Time. He could not expect to undo twenty years in one moment.

Even if he could wish it. "Surely you must exhaust yourself with all of these slings and arrows, brother. Besides, it is all very boring. If you must insult me, is it too much to ask that you come up with something new?"

"If I had wanted conversation, I would have addressed my mirror," Valentino replied coldly. "That would have provided me with far more opportunity for reflection and honest interchange than whatever games it is you think you will be playing with me tonight."

They stared at each other, all of that history between them.

"I thought you should know," Aristide said after a moment, choosing each word carefully since he could just about tell that tonight would not be the night he got through to his brother. And still, he wanted to tell him. And still, he wanted to extend this olive branch in the hopes someday it would be planted and bear fruit. "It is early days, but Francesca and I are expecting a child."

Valentino stared back at him. "Why are you telling me this?"

"I appreciate your congratulations." Aristide shook his head, almost tempted to laugh. "In the past, you have had a tendency to assume the worst, so I thought you should know. My wife and I are having a baby. It is not an assault on you, or your position as heir—whatever that means with a father such as ours. I merely thought you should hear it from me."

Valentino didn't move, except to perhaps clench his glass tighter. "It is funny, is it not, that you have anointed yourself the messenger of all of these things. That despite the reception you must expect from me, you consider it your duty to fill me in. What does that say about you, I wonder?"

"Perhaps nothing," Aristide said quietly. "But then, I am the one who trusted you to remain my friend no matter what happened. You are the one who broke that trust." Not an accusation. Just the truth of what hurt. Like Francesca had taught him.

"Your mother taught me to cook and clean as a child," Valentino said instead, abruptly. "Do you remember?"

Aristide did not understand the change of direction, but he was willing to follow it.

Olive branch, he reminded himself.

"Of course I remember. I was there."

"Why?" Valentino asked, as if he was demanding to know the whys of why life existed. "Why did she do such a thing? Was it…did she get some amusement from this?"

Aristide still did not quite know how to characterize his mother. He had seen more of her in the past few weeks than he had in the past few years, as she and Francesca always had their heads together. And he had seen her in a new light, in the way she was with Francesca, offering his wife a mother she'd never had the chance to have.

It had reminded him of all the ways his mother had been good, even if there had been quite a few mistakes she'd made that hurt him deeply. She was not perfect.

Like the rest of them, she was learning as she went.

Which meant she was no one's enemy either. "Cooking and cleaning is how my mother loves, Valentino," Aristide said, trying to be gentle. "It is how she shows her love. Not quite the villain in your story, I think. Just a woman in love. For her sins."

Valentino stood abruptly. "I commend you on your ill-gotten marriage and all the many moral lessons it will teach an impressionable child," he said. And then, "As it happens, I have also married. And I'm also expecting a child."

It hurt. Not because he wasn't happy for his brother, but because Valentino said it like an accusation. Like they were still at odds and in competition, when it should be... Aristide saw what a future *could* be. Them growing their families together, in hope and in love.

Valentino seemed to have neither at the moment, and so he wasn't ready yet. Aristide offered a wry smile. "But of course you are."

Valentino nodded. "May the cycle continue," he said, then turned on a dime and stalked away.

Aristide had finished his drink, contemplating the exchange. Still not sure why it did not hurt quite the way he'd expected. It was only when he recounted the evening to Francesca that it dawned on him.

"He was not himself. Not cool. Not calm. Not collected. I recognize the hunted look of a man not quite sure what to do with good."

"An excellent sign, then. He'll come around."

And she was right. Because Valentino did come around. With his pregnant wife, the bright and dazzling Princess Carliz, and it was clear Valentino had indeed been hunted that night. By love.

Amends were not immediate. The building of a relationship with his brother was careful, but they had both been changed by love. So it came that they found careful ways to rebuild a friendship that had been broken by young hurting hearts.

And when Milo refused to acknowledge Aristide's son as any kind of heir to the Bonaparte name—as if it would hurl that wedge back between Valentino and himself—they hadn't let him win.

It helped that Aristide was very rich on his own, of course, but neither he nor Valentino had any use for the legacy of meanness and cruelty that they had been brought up in.

It wasn't very long before Milo died, ingloriously, that Aristide and Francesca finally convinced Ginevra to move to their castle. At first, to help with their growing family.

Then, once Milo was indeed gone to hell where he belonged, and Vale suggested they turn the old Bonaparte estate into an orphanage, his mother moved there to work with the children. Francesca also lent much time to the establishment, as did their children over the years.

The Bonaparte brothers filled their island with the sound of children, of joy, of life. Something Milo would have *hated*.

But Aristide almost never thought of his own father anymore. Like Francesca had said all that time ago.

They were not their parents and they were not their pain. They got to choose.

And he had chosen his beautiful wife, his children, his brother, and love over all else.

* * * * *

Were you swept off your feet by Italian's Stolen Wife?
Then you'll love the other installments in
The Diamond Club series!

Baby Worth Billions
by Lynne Graham

Pregnant Princess Bride
by Caitlin Crews

Greek's Forbidden Temptation
by Millie Adams

Heir Ultimatum
by Michelle Smart

His Runaway Royal
by Clare Connelly

Reclaimed with a Ring
by Louise Fuller

Stranded and Seduced
by Emmy Grayson

Available now!